LONGHAIRS AND SHORT TALES

A COLLECTION OF CAT STORIES

STEFON MEARS

Thousand
Faces
Publishing

Published by Thousand Faces Publishing, Portland, Oregon

http://1kfaces.com

Front cover image © Fedor Labyntsev | Dreamstime.com (File ID: 44478923)

"Ask the Cats" was originally published in *Fireside Magazine* #11, March 2014

"Night of the Hogtied Alien" was originally published in *The Patreon Collection, Volume 4* from Thousand Faces Publishing, October, 2019

"The Secret of Catnip" was originally published in *Fiction River: Feel the Love*, from WMG Publishing, March 2019

"The Language of Cats" was originally published in *Uncollected Anthology* #20, *The Crossroads Hotel*, December 2019

ISBN: 978-1-948490-32-0

Longhairs and Short Tales

A Collection of Cat Stories

CONTENTS

FOREWORD

Cats have always been part of my life. Even when I had no cats of my own, neighborhood kitties would often go out of their way to make sure I got my share of feline attention. Sometimes when I went walking, sometimes around the mailbox. One little Russian blue cat even used to climb my screen door to ask me to come out and play.

One of the side benefits of all this feline attention is that I've had a lot of opportunity to study cats over the years. Their quirky behavior, their odd sort of politics, the sheer goofiness they can exhibit when they feel sufficiently safe and loved.

I've developed a lot of my own opinions and speculations about the rationales behind the weird and wild behaviors of cats, and I play a lot with such ideas in this volume.

This collection includes ten different views of cats. Magical cats, mysterious cats, mythical cats, loving cats, wise cats, and just plain weird cats. There might even be a talking cat or two.

So settle back, perhaps with your favorite little purring friend on your lap, and enjoy.

THE COFFEE CURSE

When I was a kid, one of my favorite shows was *Bewitched*. Syndicated reruns ran often in our area, and I came to love the antics of Samantha and her family and friends. (I may also have had a slight crush on Elizabeth Montgomery.)

Much as I loved that show, though, to me it was missing something critical. Where was the cat? Where was the talking, smartass feline familiar?

I always knew that if I wrote about a modern Witch, I'd have to make sure she had what Samantha Stevens was missing.

The best part about all this? I wasn't really thinking of any of it when I sat down to write this story. I just had the idea of a guy having his shower interrupted by his neighbor's cat. His neighbor's *talking* cat.

I have to say, though. If the Liz in this story is my Samantha, then I suspect that Reuben might become her Darren.

THE COFFEE CURSE

FEW THINGS IN LIFE ARE BETTER THAN A HOT SHOWER AT THE END OF A long day. Especially a day involving manual labor. All that water – just this side of scalding – beating merciful relief into sore, tired muscles while I scrubbed away sweat and grime. Replaced the stench of effort with good, clean soap and the vaguely citrus scent of my shampoo.

I think that shower had felt especially good because manual labor wasn't my thing. If I got my skin covered in sweat and my muscles sore from lactic acids, nineteen times out of twenty I'd been down the street playing basketball.

And why not? I'd loved playing it in high school and college, and it was still fun four years out of college. Did great things for keeping me in shape, too.

Alas, though, this day's efforts weren't basketball related. Nor any other fun activity I could name that might leave me sweaty, sore, or both, and I could think of a few.

No. My mom had asked me to come over for lunch. And, like a fool, I'd gone.

Don't get me wrong. I love my mom. And lunch was great. My

mom could grill cheese like nobody else I knew. But that lunch had been followed by *four solid hours* of lugging furniture around.

Most people clean in the springtime. My mom redecorates.

Scott, my older and wiser brother, hadn't been able to make it. Even my dad had a golfing date he couldn't break – club tournament time. So it was just me doing all the heavy lifting.

Mind you, I was in pretty good shape. But I was in basketball shape. Not furniture-lugging shape. Very different muscle work involved, and about two thirds of my body had been complaining before I'd popped a few ibuprofen and hopped into the much-needed shower.

I'd just gotten to my favorite part of the shower – when I'd finished cleaning myself and could just power-wash hot relief into my tired muscles, one group at a time – when I heard a voice calling me.

"Hello? Hello! Reuben?"

I gritted my teeth and killed the shower. The squeak of the handles seemed to echo my own internal complaint at being interrupted by some stranger.

And where the hell were they calling me from? Sounded practically inside ... my ... apartment.

No. Had to be a trick. Echoes of the shower stall, maybe. I was surrounded on two sides by translucent Plexiglas and four (including the ceiling and the stall floor) by yellowish tile.

I stood there, shivering and dripping and hoping I'd been very wrong to think that the voice I'd heard had been coming from inside my—

"Reuben?"

A chill washed over me that had nothing to do with the sudden loss of all that hot water.

That voice had come from just on the other side of my bathroom's sliding door. A male voice. A little high-pitched, but I couldn't tell yet if it was because the person was young, or just had a high-pitched voice. Some guys did.

I tried to tell myself that the voice sounded worried. Not threatening. But that didn't change the fact that there was still *a stranger in my apartment.*

Yeah, my heart was pounding again. Hard as it had been going when I finally got Mom's piano all the way from the living room in the front of the house to the back of the family room, at the back of the house.

Naturally, it had been the last piece to be moved.

I didn't know if I should answer the voice. Whoever was there had to have heard the water running, and me shutting off the shower.

What was worse, I wasn't exactly in the best position to receive an intruder. I was naked, wet, and shivering. And nothing I had near me was of immediate use.

I lived alone. So I didn't keep a bathrobe in my bathroom. I just dried off in the shower, and if I still wanted to wear a robe, I just waited until I reached my bedroom. My clothes were already in the hamper in my closet. Even my cell phone was charging on my nightstand.

Hell, I only closed the bathroom door when I showered, and even then, only to keep the heat in.

No, I didn't habitually leave the toilet seat up. My college girlfriend Anne had broken me of the habit.

"Reuben?" the voice called again.

I frowned then, realizing that if this person had come to rob me, they could have done it and gone. No reason to call my name. If they'd been interested in hurting me, well, the bathroom door wasn't *locked.* Just closed. They could be in here with me right now, if they wanted.

So maybe this was something else?

"Just a damn minute," I called out. "At least let me dry off."

"Please hurry? Liz needs your help."

Liz?

The only Liz I could think of was my neighbor, next door. She lived in the upstairs end unit, furthest from the stairs, and I lived in the next unit in. Didn't know her well, though. Only to say hi to. Maybe talk about the weather. That kind of thing. She'd always seemed nice enough, though. Pretty, too, and just about my age. In fact, if I hadn't known she had a boyfriend, I'd probably have asked her out months ago, when I first moved into the building. Not even necessarily on a *date* date, just to get to know her better.

But she had a boyfriend. And I didn't want to risk a misunderstanding.

Still. If she was in trouble, I'd definitely help her out.

I just hoped it didn't involve more heavy lifting. I wasn't sure how much more of that my muscles could take.

Drying off only took a moment. I didn't even take the extra few seconds I'd need to comb out my short, blonde hair.

Liz was in trouble. I could live with messy hair.

I tied the wet towel around my waist and opened the bathroom door, expecting to meet her little brother or cousin or something.

I didn't expect her little tuxedo cat to be in my bedroom. Looking up at me.

MY BEDROOM WAS KIND OF A MESS. AFTER ALL, I HADN'T BEEN expecting company. Oh, I didn't have clothes strewn about the floor, or empty pizza boxes or anything like that. But my bed wasn't made. And I had three books open on the old blue trunk I used as a nightstand. My computer desk, on the opposite wall, was covered with notes for an upcoming game of *Dungeons and Dragons*, as was my bureau.

Did smell like I needed to get around to doing my laundry, though.

Still, even at my messiest, my room wasn't so bad that I could overlook a small tuxedo cat, sitting at the foot of my bed and staring up at me with big yellow eyes.

"Hi," I said, frowning hard enough I could feel my forehead crease, but reaching out a hand so the cat could smell me. I knew that was important for dogs, but I figured it wouldn't hurt with cats, too. "You're ... Pie, right?"

"Please," the cat said, pawing the lousy brown rental carpet in his urgency. "Please come."

One time, during a practice back in college, I got hit in the back of the head by a basketball that someone had flung at high speed. It didn't just stagger me forward as I stumbled. I swear, I could hear this kind of metallic, ringing sound that made all the other sounds around me distant and fuzzy. And it wasn't so much that the gymnasium started spinning, as that I couldn't focus my eyes on anything for a few seconds.

I didn't even realized it when I fell to the hardwood floor.

Watching a cat's mouth move while I heard it addressing me in English had just about the same effect on me.

I staggered backward against the frame of the bathroom doorway. I heard that metallic, ringing sound again, and couldn't focus on much of anything.

Next thing I knew, I was sitting on the carpet, leaning against that doorframe, and the cat was right in front of me, beside my bare left knee.

"Breathe," the cat said. "You need to breath. And you need to get dressed. Please. Liz needs help."

"How are you talking?"

"Later. I promise I'll explain later. But please—"

The urgency in the cat's voice broke through my haze. Then I was on my feet and throwing fresh clothes on my body. SF Giants tee shirt, boxer briefs and gray sweat shorts. That'd be more than enough to handle the late afternoon in Santa Clara, California, during the springtime. Didn't even waste time grabbing sandals.

"Let's go," I said, grabbing my keys and phone from my nightstand and stuffing them into my pockets.

As we left my apartment, I noticed that my front door had still been closed and locked. I almost asked how Pie had gotten in, but figured the answer would just be "later" followed by more urgency.

Late afternoon sun was pretty bright, but the air was chillier than I expected as we covered two dozen paces along the pebbled concrete walkway from my front door to Liz's.

Her door wasn't open either.

"It's not locked," Pie said. "I made sure."

I frowned at the cat, but tried the handle. It opened for me. The smell of strong coffee hit me like a slap, along with the undercurrent of something burning.

Her apartment mirrored the layout of mine. Her kitchen and dining area were to the right, and living room to the left. Hallway straight ahead, with bedrooms on either side. Probably the master on the left, since mine was on the right.

I'm not ashamed to admit that her apartment was much more tastefully decorated than mine. But before I could even spare more than a glance for the décor, Pie whipped past me and to the right...

...where I could see Liz slumped forward over a round table. Must've been drinking coffee when she collapsed, because her mug had spilled, and coffee was all over the table and dripping down onto the same lousy brown carpet I knew so well. A tablet computer sat propped in front of her, somehow free of the spilled coffee. Unlike her black yoga pants or pale blue flannel shirt.

"Liz?" I said, closing the distance to her in quick strides. She didn't respond to my voice.

Liz, from what I'd seen of her, was pale under the best of circumstances. And right now, she looked downright pasty. Her skin tacky with sweat, and a dark blue tinge around her normally pink lips. Her long black hair, normally well-brushed and shiny, hung limply where it hadn't matted to her scalp.

The blue tinge around her mouth frightened me, but when I leaned in close, I could hear her breathing shallow, wheezy breaths.

"What happened?" I asked the cat, then shook my head at what I'd just done while I pulled out my phone.

"She was drinking her coffee and reading blogs when she *don't call nine-one-one!*"

Talking to a cat was weird enough. Obeying the order of a cat felt downright surreal. But I managed to stop my finger shy of the button that would complete the call. I kept the calling app open, though, as I stared disbelief at the cat.

"This isn't a call-the-doctor thing," Pie said. "Now what I need you to do is—"

"Whoa," I said. "Let me get this straight. Liz is lying there unconscious, turning blue, and you *don't* want me to call an ambulance?"

"They can't help her. Now—"

"I know she's big on herbs" – she always had some drying on her kitchen windowsill – "but this is no time for homeopathic—"

Pie leapt right up on my shoulder. It was such a sudden, surprising movement that I dropped my phone on the cheap linoleum.

"Listen to me, Reuben," Pie said. "Liz has been cursed and we're *losing critical time*. Now will you help me or not?"

As I followed the cat's bizarre instructions, I wondered if I was dreaming. It occurred to me that I might've gotten home from Mom and Dad's too exhausted even to shower. That I might've collapsed on the big couch in my living room, or possibly made it as far as my bed before falling straight into the weirdest dream of my life.

That made a lot more sense than what seemed to be happening.

I mean, my neighbor's cat interrupting my shower? And speaking English?

Now, I'd never owned a cat myself. I'd had a dog, growing up, but Sparky'd passed when I was in high school, and hadn't had any pets at all since.

But I was pretty sure that if cats had learned to speak English, I'd've seen a news article or something. I mean, even I'd heard of polydactyl cats, and how some people took them as evidence that cats were evolving an opposable thumb.

But I hadn't heard so much as a *suggestion* that they'd developed the power of human-sounding speech.

Then there was the idea that my neighbor Liz needed my help. I couldn't remember dreaming about her before, but I wouldn't be surprised if I had. She was certainly worth a dream or two. Very pretty, with those ice blue eyes and long black hair, not to mention that shapely body of hers.

Still. If I were going to have a dream that involved Liz and showering, I'd expect that dream to involve her joining me in the shower. I wouldn't expect that dream to include her cat interrupting me, so I could find Liz passed out in a pool of coffee at her kitchen table, barely breathing, with her skin turning dark blue around her lips.

Not the kind of thing I dreamed about. At least, not that I ever remembered.

So I had to admit to myself that I was awake. That I was actually standing in Liz's kitchen, using a pale green granite mortar and pestle to grind up herbs.

And that just made this whole experience even more surreal. I was using a mortar and pestle to grind herbs?

That was the kind of thing one of my characters might've done in a game of *Dungeons and Dragons*. Probably at a big oaken table. Maybe in a witch's cottage in the woods, or a wizard's lonely stone tower at the seaside.

It wasn't the kind of thing *I* should've been doing in broad daylight, on Liz's speckled Formica kitchen counter.

I didn't even know what herbs I was grinding together. Pie had asked me to open two of the cabinets above the counter, to my left, and had been moving among the shelves, bringing down small sealed plastic bags of unlabeled herbs.

Well. Some of them were herbs. Some of them were clearly roots. And I think a couple might've been porous, crumbly kinds of stone.

Either way, Pie wasn't answering questions. He was taking charge. Telling me exactly how much to extract from each baggie. Making sure I then sealed the baggies again properly.

Some things he wanted me to chop up first. Others he had me break or crumple in my fingers as I added them into the mortar. And each time, he put the baggie away again as he fetched the next one.

By the time we'd added a dozen or so things to the mortar, the smell of the ground herbs was getting pungent. And fairly pleasant.

In fact, though I still smelled the aroma of strong coffee, I noticed I wasn't smelling that burning odor anymore.

Finally, though, Pie didn't bring down any more baggies. Instead, he ripped a paper towel off of a roll – using his mouth, which had to have been some trick – and handed it to me.

I swear, I almost added the whole thing to the mixture in the mortar.

"Now," he said. "Very carefully, I want you to dip one corner of the paper towel into the spilled coffee. Not the corner I bit. Any other corner."

"Okay," I said, turning to go do so.

"Wait," he called, and didn't add more until I turned to look back at him.

I swear, that little tuxedo cat looked as though he should've had glasses to adjust as he continued.

"Do not, under any circumstances, touch that coffee."

"You think it's drugged?"

"Please, Reuben," Pie said. "Explanations will have to wait."

I nodded.

"Just dip one corner in." He watched as I went to the table and did that. "That's right. Good. Now carry it back. Carefully."

I held it off to one side, to avoid accidentally touching any coffee. Not that I could imagine how cold coffee would hurt me. I mean, even if it was drugged, clearly Liz had needed to drink it before it affected her.

"Now," he said when I got back to the counter. "I want you to tear that corner away, touching only dry parts of the paper towel. Give yourself a safe margin."

This wasn't getting any less weird, but frowning at the cat – not to mention looking at him in disbelief – had gotten old. So I just did as I was bid.

"Good," Pie said, "now drop the torn part into the mortar."

I did.

"All right. One last thing for this part." Pie gave me what I could only think of as a serious look. "Tell me the truth. Do you like Liz?"

Apparently I had at least one good frown of disbelief left in me, because I gave it to Pie then. If all of this was some cockamamie way for Liz to find out if I was interested...

"Blood of the moon, you humans make everything so complicated." He took a step closer along the counter and tried again. "I'm not asking if you're pining away for her in the wee hours of the night. I just need to know if, as a whole, you feel more positively disposed towards Liz than negatively."

"I'm here, aren't I?"

"You're here because you followed a talking cat," Pie pointed out. "And being willing to help an unconscious woman might only mean that you're a decent person. But do you like her?"

"Sure," I said, shrugging. "I mean, I don't know her very well, but she always seems nice when I run into her. And I do enjoy our little chats about nothing, around the mailbox."

"Would you consider her a friend?"

"Well, more of a friendly acquaintance, but basically. I guess."

"Good enough," Pie said. "Please spit three times into the mortar."

"Excuse me?"

"There's no time for this, Reuben," Pie said, his tail whipping viciously back and forth. "I'd just drool into the mortar myself if it would help, but it wouldn't. We've taken too long getting to this point." He puffed a sigh. "If this is going to have any chance now, it really needs to be human saliva, offered freely by a friend. And you're the closest thing we've got. So *spit in the mortar.*"

I did. Three times.

"Now," Pie said, pawing at the Formica, "take the pestle again and grind the whole mixture nine more times. Widdershins."

"Widder—"

"*Counterclockwise.*"

As I did, I wondered what it said about my life that a *cat* was apparently frustrated with my ignorance.

As soon as I finished the ninth pass, Pie was right there with a box of matches in his mouth. He dropped them onto the counter. I withdrew a match.

"Not yet," he said. He jumped up to the top of the fridge and batted at the righthand cabinet in front of him.

Or maybe that should've been the right*paw* cabinet.

Either way, I got the message and opened it. Inside were a variety of antique-looking things.

"The censer," he said, then sighed and tapped a small brass bowl with a hinged lid.

I picked it up. I chose not to point out that what I was holding did not greatly resemble the incense censers I'd seen in church, as a child. The ones the pastor had held dangling from a chain, when he used them to spread incense around the altar.

I flipped open the hinge. Inside was a bed of salt, on which sat a small, round disc of charcoal.

"Light the charcoal," Pie said.

Mind you, even I thought that was obvious, but under the circumstances I couldn't blame him for being certain.

I also thought that giving me orders was helping him hold it together. The cat seemed pretty darn stressed. Not that I could blame him. My own heart was pounding pretty hard, though that might have been as much in confusion about what we were doing than in worry about Liz.

Once I had the charcoal going, I nodded at the mortar.

"Yes," Pie said, so I picked up the mortar and tipped the strange mix into the censer.

Pie leaned forward and breathed hard onto the mixture.

He looked up at me, and I swear the yellow of his eyes seemed to glow for just a moment.

Light gray smoke trailed up from the censer. It didn't smell anything like I expected, from the pungent herbal smell I'd noticed while grinding. It smelled...

It smelled like roasted cashews. Which made me think of Christmas Eves, when I was a kid. Mom used to roast cashews, to mix them in among the homemade peppermint patties and chocolate covered peanut butter balls she put out on trays for snacks.

The smell of that burning mix of herbs, roots, and crumbly stone made me feel six years old again. The joy of Christmas time, when the break from school seems eternal, and there's nothing to do but play and have fun.

I gave Pie a confused, lopsided smile.

"Good," he said softly. "Perfect. We may still have a shot."

He jumped down from the counter and up onto the table where Liz lay slumped and unconscious. Still smiling, I followed him over, instinctively avoiding the spilled coffee.

"Now," he said, all business again. "Take your ... you're right-handed?"

I nodded.

"Take your right hand and use it like a fan. Waft the incense all over her, starting from her feet and working up to her head."

Sure. Why not? Incense had to do its thing, right? I didn't know what that thing was, but, good as I felt, I didn't see any point in worrying about it.

I was as thorough as I could be, given that I didn't think I should move under her to get her front side. Didn't seem right. So I focused on her back and sides. Must've done it right, too, because Pie actually murmured approval.

"Set the incense on the table," Pie instructed. "A dry spot."

I did. He put his left forepaw into the upward trail of smoke.

"Take my paw with your right hand," he said.

I did, holding that paw as gently as I could. Pie had very soft fur, but I'd been right about his claws. Even sheathed those things felt wicked.

Pie muttered some words I couldn't hear.

"Now," he said. "Touch Liz with your left hand." When I hesitated, he added, "the shoulder is fine."

I did, and noticed that she felt feverish, even through the flannel of her shirt. Pie angled himself so that his tail was touching her wrist. He muttered some more words.

That's when things got really weird. Yes, I mean weirder than a talking cat guiding me through grinding incense to help my unconscious neighbor. That was all external weirdness. But when that cat started muttering again, I ... felt something.

I don't mean emotionally. I mean physically. It was like a kind of tingling heat, spreading upward from my toes, at the same time that a kind of tingling cool spread downward from my scalp.

The sensations met around my stomach, and swirled together. Complementing, not fighting, as both continued on their routes.

Soon I felt warm *and* cool, and tingled all over, both along my skin and somehow inside me. Strangest thing I'd ever felt. And maybe it was still the influence of that happy, roasting cashews scent, but it felt good.

Then Pie looked at me again, and I startled. His eyes were definitely glowing now. Not yellow either. Burnished gold.

"Now," Pie said. "Quickly. Kiss her."

That jarred against all the good I was feeling.

"What?"

"Kiss her. Now."

"I can't do that." I shook my head. "I can't just kiss an unconscious woman."

"Think of her as Sleeping Beauty," Pie said, practically gnashing his teeth in frustration. "Wake her with a kiss."

"I won't kiss her without consent. It's wrong."

Pie's fur all puffed out. "As her familiar, I give you permission on her behalf. Kiss her."

I shook my head. "Not unless I know she wants me to."

"Think of it as giving her mouth-to-mouth."

"She's breathing."

"She won't be for long if you don't kiss her, you idiot!" Pie huffed out a breath. "Look. I'm not asking you to... Look. I'm not asking you to violate her. All right? She just needs a kiss from a friend, and you're all I've got. If it helps, on the cheek or forehead is fine."

My turn to sigh. Pie did make it sound important, but kissing an unconscious woman went against everything I believed in. I wasn't even sure kissing her on the cheek was all right.

But I had an idea of something that might be. Something that I could live with.

"Fine," I said, and while Pie told me to hurry up, I leaned down and kissed Liz gently on the back of her hand, like a courtly gesture of greeting.

Honestly, I still didn't like doing it. But I liked the idea of Liz dying even less. Especially if I could help her. I didn't see how it would, but I'd been trusting the word of a cat to this point. Seemed a little late to quibble.

As my lips reached her skin, I tasted cold coffee.

THE NEXT THING I KNEW, I WAS LYING ON A COUCH THAT WAS BOTH comfortable *and* supportive. Which meant it wasn't mine. My big ex-thrift-store behemoth was comfortable all right, but anyone who sat on it risked sinking inside, never to be heard from again.

A breeze flowing in from over my head carried spring air, and chlorine. From my apartment building swimming pool?

Yes. That would explain the sounds of kids splashing about and yelling. I could hear something else though. Someone moving around, maybe a dozen or so steps behind my head.

I opened my eyes. On the ceiling I saw the same plain white paint job that my apartment had. But the couch was high-backed, with a pattern of sunflowers against a dark blue background. Pie sat on the back of the couch, regarding me.

"He's awake," Pie announced.

"Thank you, Pye," Liz's voice called from ... the kitchen. Yes. I could hear her close a drawer. And there was something different about the way she said "Pie," but I wasn't sure what it was.

Either way, Liz's voice sounded a little strained, but pretty good for a woman who'd been – apparently – close to death.

She padded into the living room on bare feet, and the strain of ... whatever she'd been through still showed on her. Her skin still looked a bit pasty, and her hair was still a mess.

But she was alive, and mobile, and that dark blue tinge around her mouth was gone altogether. So I couldn't help smiling at her.

My peripheral vision picked up that her flannel pale blue shirt wasn't buttoned up. Instead, the ends were tied together over her midriff, just below a black sports bra. I tried not to let the sight distract me.

"Good to see you up and about," I said.

"I have you and Pyewacket to thank for that," Liz said. When she sat on the arm of the couch near my feet, I started to sit up. She immediately cautioned me with a gesture. "Don't do that. Not yet."

The wave of dizziness that hit me proved her point. I laid my head back down.

"Your ... system has been through a few shocks in rapid succession," she said. "You'll need another ... twenty minutes you think, Pye?"

"I'd advise half an hour, to be safe," Pye said.

"Half an hour," Liz continued, "before you're on your feet again."

"Will there be any lingering aftereffects?" I asked.

"Not for you," she said, in a tone dark enough that I shivered.

"What happened?" I pointed at Pye. "And why can he talk? And—"

"Slow down," Liz said, smiling, while Pye harrumphed and started bathing his forepaws. "One thing at a time. Pye can speak English because he's a familiar."

My frown of complete confusion made her smile, and that smile warmed me like the smell of roasting cashews.

Pye, however, muttered something about the low quality of American education.

"Hush, Pye," Liz said. "A familiar is a helper spirit who takes on the shape of an animal. He is my familiar, and I am his Witch."

"You say that like it should be capitalized."

"I should think so," Pye said, and Liz hushed him.

"Well," she said, "it's a religion as well as a magical practice, so, yes, I suspect I do."

"So the herbs and incense and so forth, that was—"

"Yes," Liz said, smiling even wider. "You were helping Pye cast a spell to break the curse that had been laid on me by Trevor."

"Trevor?" Man, I just could not stop frowning today. "Your *boyfriend* Trevor?"

"*Ex*-boyfriend, to be exact," she said. "As of last night. And apparently he doesn't believe any woman should survive dumping him."

"Told you I didn't like him," Pyewacket chimed in.

"Yes," Liz said, without looking at her cat. Er. Her familiar. "But you withheld that opinion until we'd been dating six weeks and—"

"At which point you decided to ignore me." Pye twitched his whiskers. "And the lesson here is?"

"Shouldn't I be asking you that?"

They glared at one another.

I cleared my throat and said, "So he cursed your coffee? That just sounds ... unfair. Coffee should be sacrosanct."

Liz chuckled and turned back to face me, smiling again.

"Nasty business," she said. "Had to have cursed the beans last night. I'll have to throw out the whole batch and buy more."

"Sloppy, too," Pye added. "Instead of just targeting you, he targeted anyone who even touched the coffee. Typical Trevor."

"I could've *died*?" I started to sit up again, heart pounding, expecting a wave of dizziness to send me right back down.

But it didn't. I sat up, blinking in surprise that I could.

"Well, will you look at that," Pye said, and I swear I heard some admiration in his voice. "Recovers quick, this one. What's it been, ten minutes total?"

"You must be in even better shape than I thought," Liz said, eyebrows high, like I'd impressed her.

"You mean for a guy who almost died?"

"No," Liz said firmly. "There was no chance of that. With the incense mixture going and Pye right there, he could've revived you himself."

"Fortunately," Pye said, "I didn't have to."

"No," Liz said. "I'll need a day or two to really feel like myself again. But no way was I going to let you suffer for trying to help me."

"You were just lucky you met Serena for coffee this morning," Pye said. "If you'd had your regular morning batch, I might not've been able to find a friend in time."

"But you did," Liz said, and turned a smile to me when she added, "Thank you."

"Happy to help," I said. "In fact, since you're out of coffee, want to go grab a cup at Boomer's?"

"Sure," she said with a pretty bright smile, all things considered. "Two conditions." She held up fingers to tick them off. "One, you let me pay. It's the least I can do."

I shrugged. "I think we kind of saved each other there, but sure."

"And two, you let me shower and change first. Right now I feel like I could scare small children at a glance."

I chuckled. "I disagree with your assessment, but I won't argue the issue. Especially since I really need to comb out my hair myself. Just knock on my door when you're ready?"

She agreed, and opened the front door for me. She gave me another smile as she leaned against the doorframe.

"I have to say, you're handling this all pretty well."

"Yeah," I said with a breathless chuckle. "Well, after meeting a talking cat, finding out about magic and curses doesn't seem so surprising."

"Fair enough," she said with a nod. But she smiled again as she closed the door.

As I was taking the short walk back to my apartment, I heard her voice, and Pye's, through their open window.

"I like this one," Pye said.

"Yeah," Liz said. "Me too."

My stomach gave a happy flutter at the thought.

FELINE GENEROSITY

My cats are indoor cats these days, because I live in an area where coyotes and raccoons are frequent passersby. But when I lived in a place where they could indulge their feral sides, I used to let them out for a while each day.

They were always well-fed enough that they didn't *need* to hunt. They did it anyway, because, well, cats are apex predators. It's what they do.

A friend of mine has a cat who brings him presents on a regular basis. Not dead animals though. Strange things. A doll. A pair of underwear. A snowshoe. He puts out little neighborhood notices, so people can come claim his cat's ill-gotten gain.

I was thinking about that that other day, and wondering what else that cat might steal, given the chance. Then I had to run to my keyboard.

FELINE GENEROSITY

When cats love you, there's a reasonable chance they'll bring you presents. Dead birds, mice, voles, squirrels, or whatever prey animal they can get their sharp little claws on.

Hard to say exactly why they do it. Might be the cat's way of contributing to the household. Might be their way of saying you don't feed yourself well enough, and they think you need assistance hunting. Could just be that they're asking you to prepare the dead thing for them the way you prepare their nightly can of wet food.

Either way, it's not very good for anybody, really. The cat doesn't end up eating the prey. The human has a mess to clean up. And while I don't think most of us mourn the death of the occasional mouse or vole, it's true that domestic cats on the hunt don't do good things for the local bird populace.

Certainly, the bird lovers seemed to be up in arms about it. My cat, Rusty – an orange tabby with reddish brown points – never brought me a single thing that had once been alive, and yet I heard loud complaints from my neighbors about what a menace he was, and how he should've been restricted to indoors-only.

Couldn't do it to him. Couldn't look into those sweet green eyes and deny Rusty the unfiltered sunlight and the myriad smells and sounds that he enjoyed every time he went out.

The way I looked at it, all cats were at least half-wild. If they didn't get the chance to indulge their feral urges from time to time, it might damage the wild part of their souls.

Of course, this was an easier call to make, living in an area where the domestic housecat had few, if any, natural predators.

I was living in Santa Clara, California, then. Temperate weather most of the year, and no serious dangers to threaten any cat smart enough to avoid raccoons. Which Rusty definitely was.

Oh, he might tease a dog or two – when safely protected by a fence – but if a raccoon came near, he came tearing back inside like the kid who just knocked over the bully's bike.

I only did that the once, in grade school. And let me tell you, I *ran*.

Anyway, Rusty loved his outdoor time, usually a couple of hours in the evening when I got home from a day spent translating techie jargon into English, and a few extra hours on weekends. My apartment was the left side of a two-story duplex, three blocks away from the nearest major street. Had only a little postage stamp yard, shaded by three huge privets, and an overabundant lemon tree. But that was more than enough territory for Rusty, most days.

He did go wandering sometimes, but never so far that he wouldn't come home when I called for him.

And he never once brought me anything dead.

Of course, my life would probably have been easier if he had. At least compared to the things he *did* bring me.

It all started during a summer heatwave. Rusty was maybe three at the time, really just coming into his own. Same could probably have been said for me. I was twenty-five then, and had just been moved up to senior tech writer, with two junior writers of my own to train and supervise.

The days were pushing three digits. I didn't have AC, so, naturally, I was worried about the little guy. I set out extra bowls of water, kept the fans running, and left frozen water bottles around my apartment to provide cool spots for Rusty during the worst of the day's heat.

When I got home in the evening, I opened all the windows and the sliding glass door into the backyard. Soon as Rusty'd devoured his dinner, he went right to the screen door and meowed for some outside time while I sat down to my own dinner – usually homemade stir-fried chicken and veggies – and decompressed with silly television for an hour or two.

Rusty would come wandering back in the early evening, ready to settle down against my thigh while I played games on my laptop.

It was a simple routine, and we followed it daily.

Somewhere along the lines of this, Rusty decided to start showing his appreciation for his outside time. Or maybe he liked the new salmon treats I'd found for him. Whatever it was, Rusty started bringing home gifts sometimes.

A stray sock caked in dried mud. Half a flipflop. The stripped handle of a golf club. Strange things like that. Always junk. Stuff I could easily just thank him for before throwing it out.

And I did thank him. Every time he did it, I said "thank you," told him he was a clever cat, and patted him on the head. Then I threw out the offering, because what was I going to do with that junk?

Especially the half-shaved Barbie head that was missing an eye. That was just creepy.

Anyway, those were the sorts of things Rusty brought me. Nothing to raise any red flags or cause any kind of concern.

At least, not until that stressful Friday.

We were behind schedule at work. That part wasn't my team's fault. That came down to the project managers accepting unrealistic timelines. But it meant everyone putting in more hours, while tempers flared all around me.

Worse, one of the junior writers under me – who shall remain nameless here for legal reasons – was discovered to have been digging around in the company database for information he shouldn't have had. And then selling that information to our competition.

So not only were we behind schedule, we lost even more time to the investigation. Plus, you know, I was worried that I'd get *fired*.

It wasn't that I'd done anything wrong. I was no part of this scheme. It's just that I was a new supervisor, and this was something going horribly wrong on my watch. For all I knew, the board might need to fire me as part of a face-saving move. Or maybe fire my whole team.

Anything to alleviate damage to the stock price, after all.

Certainly the guys in suits who kept me for over two hours answering their questions – often the same three or four questions multiple times – made the whole experience sound like a death knell for my career.

Bastards even implied that I might have to face criminal charges.

I was a mess when I got home. And Rusty, bless his little fuzzy heart, he knew something was wrong almost as soon as I came through the door.

I came through the door and straightaway flopped on the couch. The secondhand couch. A hand-me-down from my brother, the doctor, who didn't need it when he remodeled his living room.

It was sea green, and well-padded, and nicer than anything else in the house.

I could barely afford to both live and work in the Silicon Valley. And even then, I needed hand-me-downs from my brother, like I was still in high school.

I couldn't afford air conditioning. I was still driving a hand-me-down car – my parents' old gas-guzzling Pontiac Catalina – because I couldn't afford the up-front cost of replacing it with anything that cheap to keep running.

Hell, I couldn't even afford odorless cat litter. My whole apartment smelled like a great big litterbox. A clean litterbox – I scooped twice a day – but still.

If I lost my job…

I wasn't horizontal on that couch for thirty seconds before Rusty hopped up onto my chest and started purring at me.

Rusty had three different purrs. The first was his contented, sleepy purr. The one that said he was just about as happy as a cat could be and was ready to drift off to sleep. The second was his pet-me-now purr. Loud and aggressive, it was sure to pull my attention away from even the most engrossing videogame.

The third was the one he gave me then. It was a soothing purr. His way of saying, "I'm here for you, bud. We'll figure it all out together."

At least, that was my interpretation.

I poured my heart out to that sweet little cat. Told him all about everything. From the deadlines to the flaring tempers to the IP theft, finishing with my worries about criminal prosecution and loss of income.

I probably harped on that last thing the longest. I was so worried about money that night.

But Rusty calmed me down, the way he always did. Just settled in and purred at me while I petted him and talked myself out. Didn't even push for his dinner. Not until I was ready.

After his dinner, Rusty went out that night. And he brought home the last thing I could possibly have expected.

MY TRADITIONAL MEANS OF ESCAPING STRESS IS TO GRAB A TWO-LITER Diet Shasta Root Beer, heat up a frozen pizza and dive headfirst into a videogame. The more engrossing, the better.

That night pulled out all the stops. I not only brought one two-liter into the living room, I kept a second one ready in the fridge for when I needed it. I heated a three-cheese pizza with extra pepperoni, and resolved to play Skyrim until I either felt better or completed every side quest the game had to offer.

And Skyrim had a lot of side quests.

But the combination of the food, drink and game did their magic on me. By somewhere around ten o'clock I'd stopped thinking about work, money or possible criminal prosecution, and focused entirely on using magic to solve the problems of pixel people.

Right up until Rusty jumped into my lap.

Rusty's paws hit the keyboard right in the middle of a dragon fight.

"Whoa! Rust!" I cried, while trying to get his fuzzy body out of my way and salvage the fight before—

No good. My character was a dead man, and I'd have to reload from the last save point. And right then I couldn't even remember when I'd last saved.

Rusty sat on the couch next to me. Head proudly raised and tail flicking back and forth. He let loose a churring kind of meow to ensure he had my attention before he jumped down onto the thin, brown carpet.

"What?" I asked, frustrated. "You know, you—"

Then I saw what he was standing beside.

Money. Cash money. Bills folded over, held together by a thick, blue rubber band.

"What the..." I didn't bother finishing the sentence as I set my laptop aside.

Rusty gave another churring meow. Proud of himself as a hunter, the way he always was when he brought me something. No doubt waiting for my offer of thanks, his pat on the head and for me to tell him how clever he was.

I leaned down and picked up the wad of cash.

And what a wad it was. A quarter-inch thick before folding, and flipping through suggested that every bill was a one hundred.

Rusty, impatient, repeated his churring meow, and I was so stunned that I went through the thanks-pat-clever-kitty routine without thinking about it.

I was torn between counting the bills and not counting them. But I had to know what I was holding. I mean, know for sure.

I double-checked that the rubber band seemed generic, and didn't have any kind of bank markers or anything. Then I peeled it off and counted them quickly.

Sixty. There were sixty bills in this stack.

My cat had just brought me six thousand dollars in cash.

Great. I was harboring a fugitive. I might not have been part of any theft at work, but if anyone got the blame for my cat stealing six thousand dollars, I knew just where the blame would fall.

As if the heat wasn't giving me enough reason to sweat.

I don't know how long I sat there, just staring at the money. I do know that by the time I refolded the bills and put the rubber band back, Rusty had forgotten all about his theft. He was curled up in the round sleeping area on top of his cat tree, giving himself a bath.

I closed up the house. Shut and locked the glass door, closed all the windows. I even shut the drapes, some of which hadn't been closed since winter.

I went up to Rusty, who looked up and gave me a long, slow blink.

I held up the money. "Where did you get this?"

No, I didn't really expect an answer. Then again, I couldn't overlook the fact that, not four hours after listening to me drone on about money worries, my cat had come home with a fat stack of cash.

Rusty didn't answer. Unless his answer was to roll onto his back for a belly rub. He got the belly rub. I mean, what was I going to do? Punish him for bringing home something he likely didn't even understand?

I went back to the couch and stared at the folded wad on my cheap, Ikea-knock-off coffee table.

I couldn't keep it. Obviously. That would be theft.

Even though this little pack of bills represented more than I'd see in take-home pay over the next...

I actually slapped myself across the face to stop the calculations. Knowing how much money it represented to me would not help. Any more than thinking about what quality of used car I could buy with that cash, without drawing any attention to my—

What was wrong with me?

I wasn't a thief. Keeping this money would be wrong. I had to find its proper owner and get that money back.

Mind you, I wasn't looking forward to explaining how I got the money in the first place...

Maybe there was an anonymous way to give the money back?

I did rule out going to the police. Normally they would've been my first call, in a situation like that. Just tell them exactly what happened and let them figure out the rest. Hell, they might even have a procedure for dealing with large amounts of found money.

But that night, the thought of calling the police soured my stomach and sucked in my sphincter.

I might already have been under suspicion over the intellectual property theft at work. My name might already be on the police radar. And if I went to them now, maybe they wouldn't just take my word for how the money had gotten to me. Maybe they'd presume guilt.

I'd read before that police interrogation techniques could even make innocent people confess to crimes they didn't commit.

No way was I taking that risk.

No cops. I'd have to find the rightful owner myself.

That night I put the money in the inside pocket of a jacket I rarely got to wear. It was a leather, World War II style bomber jacket. I loved that jacket, but Santa Clara only got cold enough for me to wear it maybe two months out of the year. And those months felt like a lifetime away.

Can't say I slept well that night. Rusty did, at least.

The next day I went out and bought a pet cam. One of those little cameras that can attach to a cat's collar, and record his comings and goings. Didn't get the best on the market, of course, but the one I got promised four hours of recording time at 780p, which was good enough for my purposes.

Of course, buying a cat camera and *attaching* a cat camera were two different things. As a good thief, Rusty was against anything that might provide a trail of evidence.

I finally had to wrap him up in a towel like a burrito, the way I did when I trimmed his claws every few months.

Probably should've trimmed his claws first. As it was, by the time I was finished, I looked as though I'd lost a fight with a very small lawnmower.

The smell of rubbing alcohol stayed in my nose all day. Not even a good, grilled cheddar-on-sourdough sandwich drove the odor away. Had to settle for water with that sandwich. Couldn't risk going through my supply of soda too fast, not after dropping about fifty bucks on that cat cam.

Just had to hope it would pay off.

I didn't put all my hopes on the cat cam though. I also printed off a number of flyers that read *Missing something unusual? My cat might be the culprit.* And I left my phone number. That was as close as I was willing to come to asking anyone if they were missing a rubber-banded pack of sixty hundred-dollar bills.

I let Rusty go wandering close to four o'clock that day, after the worst of the heat. I probably should've waited until after dinner, but I wanted to test the cat cam, as well as get him used to wearing it.

Well, I also wanted to give him extra outside time to make up for the indignities I'd subjected him to that day. I did feel bad about that part. Wasn't as though the little guy understood what he was doing.

I had the fans going full blast, every window open, and I still felt as though I could've baked another pizza right there in the living room.

I tried to distract myself with a videogame, but it was no good. My eyes kept flitting to the glass door. Expecting any moment to see Rusty coming home again. Possibly carrying even more money with him.

I settled for watching a movie, though for the life of me I couldn't tell you what it was, or whether I liked it. It was just moving colors to stare at and sounds to pretend to listen to while I waited for the cat to come back.

My cell phone rang a few times, but no one called about money. Weirdest one was someone who thought my cat might've stolen his ten-speed bike.

Now that, I would've paid to see.

Anyway, by six o'clock Rusty wasn't home yet, so I prepared his dinner, then went into the backyard and called for him.

Maybe fifteen seconds later, he jumped up onto a neighbor's backyard fence and came strolling home along the connected fences.

He wasn't carrying any booty this time.

After he ate his dinner, I petted him into a near stupor so I could connect the cable to his collar cam and download today's first video haul.

Nothing useful. And I did watch the whole thing. In fact, I was still watching it when I let Rusty go back outside for his evening stroll.

He came back on his own before ten that night, and I watched the video of his journey before turning in for the night.

Still nothing useful. In fact, he hadn't even left the yard for the first two hours.

I sighed and settled in. This might take a while.

But surely somebody would call about the missing money.

Well, nobody called on Sunday either. Not about money, anyway. One joker did ask if my cat had stolen his wife, but I didn't even bother answering that one.

And then I had to go back to work, where I had to answer more questions about crimes I had nothing to do with. All the while fretting over the unintended crime I was all too responsible for.

Can't say I was all that productive at work, either. Which was a worry on its own. If we failed to hit this deadline and I got the blame, I'd likely end up getting fired anyway.

If I was hoping for a quick answer from Rusty, I was frustrated on that front too. He didn't leave my yard at all that night, much less revisit the scene of the crime.

And this was our pattern for the next few days. I did my best at work to hit that deadline, shorthanded, while getting interrupted at least once a day for more questions about the junior writer and the theft. In the evening I'd pretend to do something in the living room while waiting for Rusty to come back in so I could review his evening's activities.

Oh, and interspersed with all this were phone calls from randos who wanted to know if my cat had stolen a baseball card, a party invitation, a set of concert tickets (in an envelope) or a wedding ring.

Alas, I couldn't help any of these people, which just made me feel worse.

Weirdest of all, I couldn't believe no one had called about the money. There were only two reasons I could think of as to why that would be, and neither of them were good.

Either somebody hadn't noticed the missing money – meaning they had enough money to make sure their lawyers put me away for life, for daring to touch something of theirs – or the money was stolen in the first place – in which case they probably thought this was a sting. And when they found out it wasn't, well, they might decide to tie up loose ends with a .45.

My stress level was so high that week, I don't think my heart rate ever got close to normal, even during my fitful minutes of sleep. I was popping antacids like an addict, but I could still barely get myself to eat.

Hell, I bet half the reason I had to answer so many questions at work was that I undoubtedly looked guilty about *something*.

It wasn't until Saturday night that I finally had a break in the case.

I didn't even try to play a videogame that night. I just put on old reruns of *Buffy the Vampire Slayer* and parked myself on the couch while Rusty was out about his evening rounds.

Wasn't long before I collapsed into a restless doze.

When I startled awake, I assumed it was something on the television.

It wasn't. It was Rusty, sitting there in front of the couch in his proud, great-hunter pose, unleashing his churring meow to get my attention.

At his feet sat another rubber banded pack of hundred-dollar bills.

"Oh, no," I said. "Oh, no, no, no. Rusty, what did you *do*?"

He whipped his tail back and forth quickly, displeased that he was not being given his proper due for bringing me a present.

Then my poor, beleaguered, sleep-and-food-deprived bran twigged to what he'd done.

He'd repeated the same theft. *While wearing the cat cam.*

I quickly thanked him, patted him on the head and told him he was clever, then scooped him up in my arms for an extra heaping of thanks.

I'd soon have answers. I'd soon be able to put this nightmare behind me.

I closed up the house and off-loaded the footage. Skimmed quickly past the time Rusty spent lolling in my yard, then paid strict attention to where he went from there.

I got my answer in the fifth house he stopped at.

I didn't know the people who lived there, down the block from me. But now I knew that in their backyard they had a sandbox without any children's toys.

And that sandbox was where Rusty had dug up a pack of money, then proudly brought it home to me.

I almost – *almost* – went to go return the money to that neighbor. Personally, I think that was a sign of how starved my brain was for food and sleep, because I was almost to the door when I stopped and thought, *Why the hell would anyone bury packs of hundreds in their backyard?*

Maybe it was innocent. Maybe it wasn't. But now that I had proof of where the money came from, this was not my problem.

I called the police.

I expected to wait most of the night for the officers to arrive. After all, most police are pretty busy from the start of their shift straight through to the end. But I guess the amount of money involved sped up the process.

Two officers were at my house within the hour. Officer Martinez, a short but strong-looking woman, and Officer Johnson, a tall, skinny man.

I gave them the money and showed them the video. They wanted to take the cat cam into evidence, and I didn't even think to ask if I'd get it back. Just handed it over.

They thanked me, told me I'd done the right thing, and left.

First good night's sleep I'd gotten in a week.

Turned out that a bored housewife was dealing drugs, and had gotten pretty good at it. She was busted with five pounds of illegal marijuana, along with a pound of cocaine and half a pound of heroin.

Oh, and about two hundred thousand dollars buried in her back-yard sandbox.

With that behind me – and buoyed by food and sleep once more – I doubled-down at work. And not only did I not get any blame for the IP theft, I got commended for keeping the remains of my team on point and hitting that ridiculous deadline.

After the next strange phone call, asking if my cat had stolen someone's youthful innocence, I took down the flyers around my neighborhood. It was clearly time to put the whole thing behind me.

Or so I thought.

Right around the middle of December that year, I pulled my bomber jacket out of the closet and rediscovered that first pack of six thousand dollars, cash.

Apparently I'd been in bad enough shape, when I spoke to the police that summer, that I'd fixated entirely on the cash in front of me and forgotten about the cash from before.

I frowned at that wad of money for a moment, torn between just keeping it and turning it over to the police.

Rusty made the decision for me. He came up and rubbed against my leg, and gave me his churring meow, as though to remind me that the money was a present, gosh darn it. And I kept so few of his presents as it was...

I picked up Rusty, nuzzled him with my chin, and said, "All right, all right. You win. I'll keep the money."

Rusty gave me his contented purr.

THE LANGUAGE OF CATS

I once drove halfway across the country to bring a cat to a friend.

I drove an ancient 280ZX that was not in great shape. It lost its speedometer somewhere along the drive. Also, a dead turtle got lodged in the undercarriage. But trickiest of all, the cat's tolerance for the trip went only so far.

I stopped for the night three times along the way. Each morning, the sweet little thing tried desperately to convince me that we were home now, and we didn't have to get back in the car.

Thinking back on that drive got me wondering. What if some guy was taking a drive like that one to go back to an ex-? And what if that was a really bad idea? And what if the cat was trying to tell him this, but couldn't figure out how?

I wrote this story to make use of a *Twilight Zone* kind of setting called the Crossroads Hotel, as part of the *Uncollected Anthology* series. Which gave me an excuse to throw magic into the mix, and let the story run wherever it wanted.

I always love it when stories tell me where they're going, instead of vice-versa.

THE LANGUAGE OF CATS

The rain came down so hard it slowed my windshield wipers. They creaked and struggled to move that much sheer weight of water.

The worst was when some long-haul semi came roaring past me, flinging enough to drown a herd of horses.

Every time that happened – at least once every minute or so – I lost all visibility for three or four eternal, heart-stopping seconds. Always felt as though some other car would pick that exact moment to careen into my lane, or slam on their brakes, or something equally fatal.

I was on the freeway somewhere between Bakersfield and Flagstaff. No idea what time it was. The clock was broken in my ancient 280 ZX – so old it was technically a Datsun with an engine made by Nissan. The car was older than the cat in my passenger seat, and that cat had to be pushing a decade pretty hard.

Sweet little thing. Curled up in her fluffy yellow blanket, tucked into the bucket seat, and enjoying what little my heater could do to drive away the night chill. Her food and water were wedged between the front seats for easy access, and her litter box was down in front of the seat, but she just lay there. Looking at me. Trusting me to keep her safe.

Deena had named the cat Pepperhead for the black flecks sprinkled through her gray fur. Terrible name for a cat, but Deena hadn't been any older than thirteen when Pepperhead was a newborn kitten – a good six years before I met either of them – so I never disparaged the name aloud.

I was driving from San Jose to ... some little "college" town in Oklahoma, bringing Deena her cat, whom I'd retrieved from her sister, Crystal, in Gilroy.

Assuming we survived the drive, that was.

I slammed my horn in frustration at the latest semi driver trying to kill me, but the horn was broken, so my protest never registered.

Did help though. Gave me a split-second's expression of that mélange of fear and anger that had been carbonating my adrenals for the last hundred miles or so.

If muscles could sing with tension, then my entire body was somewhere in the middle of the second act of *The Ring of the Nibelung*.

Well, I suppose my stomach muscles might not have been. They were too busy complaining that I hadn't eaten since noon. Which had to have been at least eight hours ago. Worse, the lingering aftertaste of salt and grease from that last fast food stop wasn't just irritating on my tongue. It seemed to frustrate my stomach with the false promise of more.

I'd planned not to stop for the day until I reached Flagstaff, but hungry, tired, and facing steady bouts of blind panic was no way to drive.

Only problem was that the exit I'd passed a dozen miles or so prior was supposed to be the last stop for a hundred miles or so.

That meant another eighty-odd miles of creeping along in the slow lane of two, getting hammered by rain and overwhelmed by semis. Be lucky if I made that exit in less than ninety minutes. Luckier still if I made it in one piece.

The tension in my neck had gotten bad enough that even

checking my side mirrors gave me an ache. And somewhere in there I'd started clenching my jaw too tight.

That was it. I needed to pull off before I killed us both.

Pepperhead must've picked up on my tension. She let out her frustrated yowl. The one she made when a toy got stuck under the couch or coffee table, out of reach.

Another semi roared past, blaring his own horn to add insult to invisibility. I let out a yowl of my own, praying that the road would stay straight and that that Honda a few hundred feet ahead of me stayed steady.

My wipers finally cleared the latest tsunami.

And suddenly there was an exit.

Couldn't read the sign. Wasn't lit. But I could tell it was green and surrounded by a white border, like a real exit sign. And it was right beside an offramp.

I think I uttered a prayer of thanks to whatever gods might have been watching over me as I turned on my signal and pulled the hell off that deathtrap of a freeway.

The offramp seemed eternal.

Living in the Bay Area, cloverleafs were a part of my daily life. I knew them well. They were tight curves that didn't need more than a few hundred feet to get drivers onto the right exit or entrance.

This one, though, it just kept going. It had this gentle grade of turn to the right, just one lane. And between the darkness and the rain I couldn't see anything but the bleak cone illuminated by my headlights. I just kept my eyes on the road.

More specifically, I kept my eyes on the reflectors on the outside part of the lane, to keep myself oriented even through the struggles of my windshield wipers.

But the curve just kept going. Way longer than it should have. I mean, maybe I couldn't see exactly where I was or what was around me, but I wasn't completely without a sense of direction. And I felt as though I had to have turned at least two complete loops by the time I finally found myself dumped onto a straightaway.

Then again, stressed as I was, even in the moment I knew I might not have been the best judge. Might just have been a normal clover-leaf that *felt* longer than it should've, just like the water dump of every semi did.

Either way, I was on a straightaway, and that had to be worth something.

A straightaway in a closed town, by the look of things. Hardly any streetlights. The four nearby gas stations, all closed. No fast food joints either, which brought a protest from my stomach.

Motels, though, it had. A row of them down either side of the wide street. Weird that the street was so wide, after that single-lane cloverleaf. But wide it was. Two lanes each direction. Quiet, too. My car was the only car throwing sheets of water off the asphalt as I made my slow way down, looking for that all-important vacancy sign.

My windshield wipers continued to groan as they worked, but the combination of slower speeds and a lack of semis meant I could actually *see* the motels I was passing.

More specifically, I could see their full lots and their brightly lit no-vacancy signs.

By the time I passed the sixth lot full of RVs, SUVs, and miscellaneous Vs, I was on the verge of just pulling over and falling asleep behind the wheel.

Then I saw it.

A lit vacancy sign.

It was at the very end of the street, on the other side of what would otherwise be a T-intersection. The Crossroads Hotel.

I wanted a motel, not a hotel. Just a place to rest for a few hours and keep Pepperhead dry without breaking my wallet. But it looked as though I were out of options.

I pulled into the driveway, which seemed more like some kind of red running track than proper asphalt or tarmac. But boy, it kept itself clear of rain as I passed the parking lot and pulled into the circle, under the overhang.

Tan stucco building, maybe eight stories tall. Red, curved tile roof. Put me in mind of the kind of places you'd find on the Mission Trail, even though we were nowhere near that part of California.

I think my joints squeaked louder than the door of my Z when I finally got out. Yeah, I was only twenty-three, but I'd been behind the wheel for at least ten hours. And my little Z didn't have anything so fancy as an automatic transmission or cruise control.

I was cold in my cargo shorts and SJ State tee shirt, but I had to take a moment and stretch before I did anything else.

"Good evening, sir. Checking in?"

I looked up, expecting to see some bellhop my own age, but this big guy was dressed too nice for a bellhop. I swear he was wearing a tomato red tuxedo. And he was two or three *times* my age. Not that he didn't carry his years and his weight pretty well. The gray at the temples of his otherwise short, blackish hair even lent him a distinguished air.

But man, it was weird getting "sir-ed" by someone his age.

"No thanks," I said, waving away the valet ticket he held out in one gloved hand. "I'll park it myself. I just wanted to keep my cat dry while I check in."

"No problem there, sir," the valet said with a gentle smile. "The valet parking is mandatory, but complimentary for all guests of the Crossroads."

I frowned. "You'll leave it here while I check in, though. I mean—"

"I assure you, sir. Your car and your cat will be just where you expect them on your return."

His turn of phrase made me frown even deeper, but I handed over my keys, took the valet ticket, and turned to go inside and see just what this night out of the storm was going to set me back.

Inside, the place was kind of homey. Smell of cinnamon, apples and honey was the first thing I noticed.

Well, maybe not the first thing. The first thing was probably the warmth from the fireplace off to my right. Great big stone-and-mortar hearth, like something I'd've expected in a castle. The fire roaring in that hearth threw out so much warmth I think my skin had a heat-gasm. I just stood there a moment, a good two-dozen feet from the flames, soaking in the warmth.

The hearth was part of a sitting area. Big brown leather sofas were angled to half-face the fire and half-face each other, with a big wooden coffee table between them.

The floor wasn't what I expected either. Carpeting, instead of Spanish tile. Red, with gold and silver swirls in some kind of pattern. Support pillars did have the sort of tan and dull red tiles I'd figured would be on the floor, but that seemed the extent of the Mission Trail styling.

While my skin might have implored me to stand closer to the fire, my stomach begged me to turn toward the signs for the restaurant and bar – off to the left as I'd come in – but no way was I leaving poor Pepperhead out in the car in weather like this, just so I could feed my face.

The front desk was straight ahead of me, between the pillars. It looked to have been carved from the trunk of a single huge tree, with the top being smooth and lacquered, and the side facing me still covered in thick, dark bark with stubs where branches must've been.

Behind the desk was a smiling Latina woman in a red tuxedo that matched the valet's. Her black hair sat atop her head in a style so complicated I immediately wondered if she could take it down for sleep with less than an hour's effort.

"Checking in?" she asked, and I swear her tone sounded a lot like the valet's. Like maybe his voice was a little high, and hers was a little deep, so they matched in the same way their clothes did.

"If I can afford your cheapest room," I said, shaking my head as I approached.

"I'm sure that won't be a problem, sir," she said with a smile. "Our off-season rates are quite reasonable."

Despite the storm, it was late spring. I wasn't sure that qualified as "off-season," but I wasn't going to argue.

What was even a small stroke of luck, not only didn't she charge me a pet fee for bringing Pepperhead, she actually gave me a discount for traveling with a cat.

"The owners are devout animal-lovers," she said with a smile.

"They like to encourage those who love animals enough to travel with them. Are you, perchance, rescuing this cat?"

"Well," I said, struggling between poverty and honesty, "not really. I'm returning Pepperhead to her proper person, Deena Paulson, from her sister's house."

"Close enough," the kind lady said with a wink, and knocked another ten percent off my rate.

"I'm afraid the restaurant is closed for the night, Mr. McCleary," she said as she handed me my key – an actual old-style brass key – "but you can still get food service in the bar, if you're hungry."

I'm pretty sure I turned bright red with embarrassment at that. I hadn't asked about food, so she had to have heard my stomach's complaints. I turned away quickly to go collect Pepperhead and my overnight bag.

When I stepped back outside to pick up Pepperhead, a bellhop was waiting for me. She couldn't have been older than eighteen, and from her features I would have believed her if she told me the valet and the desk lady were her parents.

More disturbing to me, though, was that she hadn't just taken my overnight bag out of the hatchback. She'd loaded up her bell cart with my two suitcases, plus my four cardboard boxes, as well as everything but Pepperhead and her things.

"You unpacked my car," I said.

"Bell service is complimentary for all guests of the Crossroads," the bellhop said. Her voice might have been a little higher than her mother's – if the desk lady was, in fact, her mother – but she had that same odd quality to her voice at both the valet and the desk lady. I couldn't quite place what it was, though, so I wrote it off to being tired and strung out from the road.

And she didn't seem to be getting my point.

"But you unpacked my *whole* car," I said.

"It is the policy of the Crossroads that nothing valuable be left in the parking lot," she said, still smiling despite my clear discomfort.

I sighed and let my head sag. Beaten by bureaucracy again.

"Well," I grumbled, "at least that shouldn't keep my *car* out of the parking lot." Louder, I said, "Fine. Let me get Pepperhead though."

"Of course, sir. Your cat is just where you expect her."

I just couldn't even comment on that one. I opened the passenger door and scooped up Pepperhead in her blanket. Pepperhead reached out and nuzzled my chin, purring as though her faith in me had never wavered.

"She's adorable," the bellhop said. "Would you like me to retrieve her food, water and litter? Or would you rather?"

"I'll just carry her, if you don't mind."

The bellhop's smile brightened. "It's better that way."

THE VALET LED ME TO ROOM 237, WHERE SHE EASILY STACKED MY THINGS in a neat pile – apparently the woman was stronger than I was, and while I was no weightlifter, I was in decent shape – refused a tip, and left.

As I took in the room, I wondered how the hell this place stayed in business. They charged me less than I would have paid for a room in a chain motel. But this room. This huge room…

The carpeting was thick, and soft. And it wasn't the usual kind of hotel color that hides stains. It made me think of the kind of foam that got caught in tide pools sometimes, up in Half Moon Bay.

The walls were a subtle, sandy color, somewhere between red and yellow, just rough enough under my fingers to continue the beach theme in my head.

It was heated by a red coral fireplace that looked to have been burning driftwood.

The desk under the bay window seemed to have been made from driftwood, as did the chair before it, and the coffee table over in front of the couch, by the fireplace. The couch itself had something familiar about it, but I couldn't place what. It was a dark brown, over-stuffed beast.

The comforter on the king-size bed was dark brown as well, with an orange diamond pattern in the center. The nightstands on either side of it continued the driftwood theme, and the lamps on those nightstands looked to have been made from seashells.

The overhead lamp's shade looked like a starfish, with its legs half-coiled as though it were moving.

Only the red digits of the nightstand clock looked ordinary. Even the phone on the desk had a vaguely seashell look to it.

There was a slight honey and peanut butter scent to the air that was driving my stomach mad. The scent was familiar, too, but I couldn't place it just then.

"What do you think, Pepperhead?" I asked.

Pepperhead jumped from my arms onto the back of the couch, then down onto the seat, where she took her rightful spot in the center, directly in front of the fireplace.

"So you approve then," I said, chuckling. I turned to make sure her water and food were set up right, but only then noticed that Pepperhead's food and water bowls were already on the carpet, near the fire. I shook my head. "Bet your litter pan's already in the bathroom."

Instead of checking, I settled on the couch next to Pepperhead and gave her lots of petting and scritching for a while, making sure she was good and settled.

Then I could deny my stomach no longer.

"Okay," I whispered to the cat, "I'm going to grab something to eat. Be sure to stretch your legs a bit, huh? I know the fire feels good after that cold car, but I'd feel better if I knew you'd gotten a little exercise."

Pepperhead, as a proper cat, didn't deign to acknowledge my words.

I eased off the couch, double-checked the litter pan – already in the spacious bathroom, positioned between the bidet and the far wall – and made my way down to the bar.

I half-expected the bar to be empty when I got there. The hotel just seemed so quiet, whether I was in the halls, the elevator, or the lobby. But it turned out there *were* other guests at the Crossroads that night.

The bar was more of a lounge than anything I thought of as a bar.

Lots of round tables surrounded by padded, leather chairs. Smell of hickory and cherry wood coming from the fireplace off to the left – geez, did *every* room in this hotel have a fireplace? I'd have to remember to look for all the chimneys when I left.

Hardwood floor in here. Something dark and chocolatey, same as the bar itself, off to the right. The walls were painted with subtle murals depicting old, dirt crossroads in different kinds of environments.

A handful of suits sat on stools up at the bar, while the men and women wearing them laughed and drank and told each other stories. One of the nearby tables had a couple too involved in each other's eyes to even bother drinking their glasses of white wine. Or touching their cheese platter, for that matter. In the back left corner of the room, a big, African-American Hell's Angel type stared into his mug of beer between sips.

"Grab a seat anywhere," called the bartender. A young man about my age, who looked as though he could have been the bellhop's brother. Like the other Crossroads' employees I'd seen so far, he wore a red tuxedo.

His voice did stand out a little from the other three though. Held a little more variation to its tone. I actually wondered if that meant anything while I found a table that didn't feel too close to the suit crowd at the bar, but still far enough away from the couple and the Hell's Angel to give them space.

Just as I sat down, the bartender reached my table and handed me a menu.

"Heard you might be hungry," he said with a smile. "Anything to drink while you—"

"Do you guys have burgers?" I asked, not looking at the menu.

"Of course," he said, and didn't take a single note as I ordered a bacon double-cheeseburger with onion rings and whatever diet cola they had, as long as he didn't soil it with ice.

While I waited for my food, I closed my eyes and relaxed. Tried to let the raucous suits and their stories and jokes wash over me, without trying to listen for details. I was just glad to have the company. The sound of human laughter and voices. That drive had been so isolating, I'd started to feel as though Pepperhead and I were the last two living beings on earth.

The drivers of those semis didn't count, after all. They were clearly demons from the pit sent to torture me for reasons unknown.

Maybe it had just been too long since I'd eaten, but the food, when it came, was *incredible.* The burger was juicy and perfect, the cheddar cheese melted just right, and the pepper bacon gave the whole thing an extra kick of spice that was just what the doctor ordered. The onion rings were crispy and delicious, and the bartender threw in a slice of chocolate cake – on the house, no less, "for surviving that storm" – and that cake was good enough that I still remember it in dreams sometimes. Creamy and thick and wiping away even the memory of grease from the burger and rings.

The couple left before I was halfway done with my burger. They'd never touched their wine or cheese – far as I could tell from where I sat – but from the way they looked at each other as they hurried out of the lounge, they didn't care in the least.

The biker left while I was finishing my cake. From the patch on the back of his leather vest, he was in some kind of gang or club. Something called the "Transmaniacon MC."

The suits at the bar were still going strong when I made my way to the elevator, feeling good. Good food in my system had given me a real lift, and combined with the stories and laughter, I was smiling as I stepped off the elevator onto the second floor.

Smiling right up until I saw that the door to my room was open.

Panic washed over me as I ran into my room. While not *everything* I owned was in there, most of the things that really mattered to me were.

Only took seconds, though, to realize no one had stolen my meager possessions. My boxes were still there. My suitcases too, and my overnight bag. All right where the bellhop had left them. And no one could have stolen my cash, because that was in my wallet. I patted my left front pocket out of reflex, and the wallet was right where it was supposed to be.

I sank to my knees in relief. My heart lurched and started slowing back to something like its normal rate. My overtensed muscles from that rough drive now felt as though they were ready to snap, and—

Where was Pepperhead?

I scrambled back to my feet so fast I pulled a hamstring and had to limp over to the couch to check on Pepperhead...

...who was not on the couch. Nor was she curled up on the floor closer to the fire, nor snacking on her food, nor drinking from her water bowl...

She wasn't *on* the bed. She wasn't *in* the bed. She wasn't *under* the bed.

No luck in the bathroom, either, or around the desk.

I clucked my tongue the whole time, just the way I always did to get her attention. It was usually more than enough to get Pepperhead to come out of hiding for some attention. And by the time I'd checked the whole room twice, I was sure either she'd gotten out or someone had taken her.

I left the room then, triple-checking to make sure I locked it this time. I mean, I was pretty sure I'd locked it last time, but tired and strung out as I was, I must not've.

Out in the hall, I looked both ways, hoping to see a little gray cat flecked with black. But nothing on the floor of the hall but the red carpeting, with its gold and silver swirls.

The walls of the hallway were a nondescript tan stucco, with no shelves to jump onto, nor tables to hide under. The alcove with the ice machine was only about twenty feet away or so, near the elevator.

Could she have gotten on the elevator?

I limped over and pressed the call button. Got the elevator I'd just been on. Checked anyway – empty – then sent it up to the sixth floor and called the elevator again.

No cat in the other one either. If I didn't find Pepperhead soon I'd have to call the front desk. See if the staff could help me look.

I checked next to the ice machine, but she wasn't there. There was an unlabeled door beside it that I assumed was for the maintenance staff or the cleaners, but it was locked.

I knocked anyway, and called through it, but when I didn't hear any muffled Pepperhead sounds, I turned away, frustrated.

"My own fault for telling her to get some exercise," I muttered. Yes, I knew that was ridiculous. I mean, even if cats spoke English, what were the chances they'd take health care advice? But I wasn't quite at my most stable, and I was still trying to persuade myself that the cat was missing, not taken.

As I left the alcove, I heard a woman's voice down the hall. I didn't see anyone in the hall, but I had to check.

Grimacing at the discomfort, I trotted down the carpet, and quickly spotted an open door at the end of the hall, on the right. I picked up the pace, despite protests from my hamstring.

Pepperhead mattered more. I could rest later. I kept going.

The hall, like that eternal cloverleaf earlier, seemed longer than it should have while I tried to reach that open door. I actually broke a sweat and had to slow down before I got there.

In some ways, that was the weirdest thing to happen to me all day. I mean, I was a guy who played basketball four times a week, for hours at a time. There were stronger guys out there, but stamina I had in spades.

I should not have been panting for breath when I reached the end of that hall. But I was.

I wiped sweat out of my eyes and ignored the throb from my thigh as I knocked on the doorframe.

"Come in, Mr. McCleary," the woman's voice said, a smoky contralto that seemed to invite with its tone as much as its words.

I frowned at being identified by name. Still, the voice intrigued me.

The room bore a superficial resemblance to my own, only in its approximate size, and that it had a fireplace, a desk, a couch and a king-size bed. Where my room was decorated in a beach theme, this one seemed done like a cabin in the woods.

Wide, pale orange boards that looked like tree trunks for the floor and walls. Stone and mortar hearth. White fur bedspread on the bed. Desk made from the same kind of wood as the floor, and its chair matched the couch – apparently handmade and unpadded.

The owner of the voice sat on the couch before the fire. I couldn't guess her age. I knew she was older than me, but whether the age difference was five years, ten, or twenty, I couldn't come close to knowing. Her skin was pale, and so smooth I doubted she'd ever *seen* a pimple, much less had one. Her hair, a deep bloodred that hung loose down past her shoulders to at least her elbows.

She wore dark green slacks, and a green plaid felt shirt that brought out a pale green in her eyes as she turned to look at me, smiling.

Pepperhead was curled up in her lap, purring.

The sight of Pepperhead filled me with such relief I slumped against the doorway.

"She's all right," I mumbled.

"I daresay," the woman said, still smiling. "And I think you'll find the couch a good deal more comfortable, if you'd like to sit."

"Please," I said, and did make it to the couch before slumping down. Despite the lack of padding, the couch actually was fairly comfortable.

It's funny, though. Maybe it was the long day, or the exhaustion, or just the stress of worrying about Pepperhead, but this woman's beauty barely registered with me. I noticed that she was beautiful, but only to the extent that it was another detail about the room. Fireplace, check. Fur blanket on the bed, check. Occupant beautiful enough to outshine movie stars, check.

"It seems you've had quite a day, Mr. McCleary," the woman said. "Or may I call you Brice?"

I nodded, slowly, still wondering how she knew my name. "And you are?"

"You may call me Brenna," she said, holding out her hand to shake. She had a good grip, and I noticed that even while shaking hands, she continued petting Pepperhead.

"I see you've already met Pepperhead."

"Oh, dear," she said, and I swear she was talking to the cat, "I'd hoped you were kidding about that." To me she said, "You actually call her Pepperhead?"

"Not my fault," I said. "Deena named her."

"Yes, Deena," Brenna said with a small frown. "Who banished you, then abandoned this poor dear."

"Well, *banished* and *abandoned* are strong words," I said before I realized what I was saying. "Wait, how do you—"

"Anyone with the proper natural inclinations can understand the speech of cats," Brenna said with a hint of mischief, "though it does take patience. And sometimes the right opportunity. This one here" – she scritched Pepperhead under the chin and cooed her last words to the cat – "is quite talkative. Aren't you?"

I was torn between saying something like "Oh, come *on*" and making an excuse to take Pepperhead and leave, when Brenna gave me a sly smile.

"She's quite fond of you, though," Brenna said. "She assures me that you were more worried about her than you were about yourself, even driving through such horrible conditions."

"I—"

"Though she doesn't think much of your car. The seat was comfortable enough, but the heater, most inadequate."

"Hey!"

"And she hopes you aren't going back to Deena. Because she's quite convinced Deena will hurt you again."

"Okay," I said, gesturing with both hands for Brenna to stop for a moment. "Lotta stuff in my room. Too much for a guy just bringing back a cat. Maybe you saw."

"I didn't—"

"And maybe you saw me pull up in the Z." I shook my head, but Brenna didn't interrupt me this time. "But how could you possibly know anything about Deena? I haven't said her name since I got here."

"No," Brenna said. "*You* haven't."

I looked down at Pepperhead then back up at Brenna.

"Oh, come on."

"Then how do I know that the first time you met this sweet little one, you apologized to her for the name?"

"Who wouldn't?" All right, most of my friends wouldn't. In fact, a lot of people thought the name was cute, and fit the cat. Didn't mean they were right.

"And how would I know that you whispered that apology quietly, so as not to hurt Deena's feelings?"

"Well—"

"Brice, let us set the language of cats aside a moment and discuss what matters."

"What would that be?"

"This little one doesn't wish to go back to Deena. Deena was good to her as a kitten, true, and Pepperhead, as you call her, is grateful. But Deena has been less and less attentive as Pepperhead has grown older. The abandonment was the final straw."

"Deena wants her back," I said carefully. "And she's Deena's cat."

"She's her own cat, thank you very much," Brenna said. "But I'll let that slide because I know you mean well. And be honest, did Deena propose your bringing Pepperhead to her? Or did you?"

I didn't bother answering. Truth was, *I* was looking forward to having Pepperhead around again.

"I thought as much, and so did Pepperhead."

"So I suppose Pepperhead wants to live with you?"

"Not at all," Brenna said. "She'd much rather live with you again."

"But—"

"If you take her to Deena, she will run away."

"She ran away from me tonight."

"Not at all. She came to me because she felt the presence of one who could translate."

Felt the presence? One who could translate?

I was too tired for this crap.

"Running away would be a terrible option," I said, getting caught up in the idea that Pepperhead could literally understand not just my tone but my words. "Even an imperfect home is better than the feral life. She's not a kitten anymore."

"Exactly what I said," Brenna said with a smile. "Which is why, if you will refuse her, I think she should stay here at the Crossroads. And I believe she is willing to do so."

"Here."

"Certainly. The owners love animals, and the staff would dote on a hotel cat. Warm fires in every room. And she'd be well fed and taken care of. She'd miss you, though."

"I don't think I could just ... *take* Deena's cat. Wouldn't be right."

"We'll come back to that. What's this Pepperhead tells me about you going back to Deena?"

"*So* not relevant," I said, making my way to my feet. My knees cracked, and my hamstring tried to sue for abuse, but I got my feet under me.

"It's a mistake," Brenna said, undaunted. "Deena may be saying the right things right now, but she won't be faithful."

"And how would *you* know?"

"I don't," Brenna said. "But this little one tells me Deena cheated more than you know. To name only one of several, she recommends that you ask about Roger."

Roger? He was one of my best friends at San Jose State. Hadn't seen him much since graduation, but...

Roger and Deena?

A little voice in my head whispered that it might be true.

"Enough," I said. "I'm going back to my room. And I'd like to bring Pepperhead with me..."

The words were barely out of my mouth before Pepperhead jumped down and meowed at me.

The timing of that was...

"I should make you walk back to the room," I said. But I didn't. I picked her up. To Brenna I said, "Thank you for looking after her."

"My pleasure," Brenna said with a smile. "As was meeting you."

I wanted to say "likewise," but couldn't quite bring myself to say it.

I turned to leave, but before I got out the door, though, something else occurred to me.

I stood there in the doorway a moment.

"You said Pepperhead came to you."

Brenna, standing only a few steps away, nodded, smiling.

"Then how did she get out of my room?"

"The Crossroads won't hold anyone against their will."

I hate answers that only give me more questions. But I knew – I just *knew* – that if I asked Brenna any of those questions, I wouldn't get any answers I'd believe.

―――――――

THE WALK BACK TO MY ROOM DIDN'T SEEM SO FAR, WHICH WAS GOOD news for my hamstring. And once back in my room, I went straight to bed.

Not to sleep, though. Oh, no. Even so exhausted I could cry, and sprawled on a bed that was more comfortable than the one I had back at my parents' place, my mind whirled in a cyclone that gave me no peace.

Talking cats. Strange, witchy women. Cheating exes. Disloyal friends. Hotel rooms with minds of their own...

Finally I couldn't take it anymore.

I sat up, threw off the bed coverings and flipped on the nightstand light.

Across the room, on the desk, Pepperhead hunched beside the phone, staring at me. Her reflected eyes seemed to glow green.

"Fine," I said, getting up and stomping across the room. "I'll call."

Absently I petted Pepperhead as I dialed Deena's number.

Took her five rings to pick up, and her voice slurred with sleep as she said, "Hello?"

I had to swallow hard – why was my heart beating so fast? – before I could even manage a "Hi."

"Brice?" she asked, coming more awake with every word as she continued. "Do you know what time it is?"

"No," I said, refusing to look back at the clock to find out. "But I do know I just have a very interesting conversation with Roger. Care to guess what about?"

I held my breath and crossed my fingers.

"Well, shit," Deena said. "Look, Brice. It didn't mean—"

I hung up. I knew all the words and movements to that song and dance too well to bother with them again.

I called the front desk and put the line on do-not-disturb. While I was doing that, Pepperhead pushed against my hand with her nose, and pressed against my side with her hip.

"Come on," I said, picking her up. "Let's get some sleep and figure it out in the morning."

When I woke up hours later, Pepperhead was curled up on my chest, purring happily.

I felt like crap. My thigh was barking at me. My neck and shoulders were a mess from the stress of last night's drive. Worst of all, I felt stupid and heartsick, and had no idea what the hell I was going to do next.

But that little purring cat on my chest still made me smile. A wistful smile, but still. There was just something about the pure love of that little creature that reminded me that there was still good in the universe. There was still hope.

I reached out to scratch that spot behind her ears, and Pepperhead stretched one forepaw and pressed it against my chin, her claws only coming out enough to dent my skin.

She gazed at me with slowly blinking eyes.

"Good morning," I said. And I admit, I was half-surprised I didn't get a response. The way things were when I fell asleep last night, I'd started to believe she really could not only understand me, but communicate clearly right back to me.

I sighed when she didn't.

"Well," I muttered, scratching her cheeks and neck now, "obviously I can't go on to Oklahoma and Deena. Do I bring you back to Crystal?"

Can't I stay with you?

I didn't hear a voice. No one speaking English words. And yet, as I looked into Pepperhead's eyes, I swear that thought just ... appeared in my head. And it didn't feel like one of *my* thoughts, either.

"Was that you?"

Pepperhead reached out and nuzzled my hand.

"That's a yes, isn't it?"

She did it again. I chuckled.

"All right," I said, and took a deep breath as I considered whether or not I was finally going insane. "But I don't know where I'm going. I mean, obviously I'm not going on to Oklahoma. But I couldn't stand going back to my parents' place either. Not that they'd let me take you in. I just—"

Sean?

Sean. My oldest friend in the world, even if I didn't get to see him much these days. I'd been a junior when he'd decided not to transfer from his community college to a four-year, and instead moved to L.A. to take a crack at screenwriting.

"Sean," I said slowly. "He'd take me in, no questions asked. For a while, at least." I smirked and patted Pepperhead. "He'd take you in too, but you knew that already. Didn't you?"

Another nuzzle.

"Yeah, Sean never cared much for Deena, but he did like you, didn't he? All right. I'll give him a call after I grab something to eat downstairs, then we can head out and be at his place ... oh ... maybe before dark."

Pepperhead purred, but showed no inclination to get off my chest.

"You realize you'll have to move to make this happen."

Nothing but more purring.

"Oh, and since you aren't any happier about my calling you Pepperhead than I am about doing it, how about I call you something else? What do you think of Andromeda? It's a little hoity-toity maybe, but—"

Andromeda nuzzled my hand, twice, then got down so I could get dressed and seek out my breakfast.

And after that, a new direction for my life.

LONG WAY FROM HOME

It's hard for me to write an introduction to this one without spoiling the story. I'll do my best.

I always feel a little sad when I see posters for lost animals. I stop and look around for them, and try to stay aware for possible sightings while passing through the neighborhood.

I haven't seen any such notices lately, for which I'm grateful. But I was thinking about lost animals all the same, and I wondered who might be the best person to find the most lost cat I could think of.

I need to stop talking about this story now, or risk ruining it.

LONG WAY FROM HOME

The falling snow was colder than Abby's heart.

All right. Maybe that was just my heartbreak talking. Wasn't her fault that it started snowing just after she dumped me. And honestly, she didn't have that bad a reason.

Abby was a marine, and looking at a six-month tour overseas that started tomorrow. We'd only been together four months. Simple Abby math said that we'd never survive being apart that long, so why try? Better to rip the Band-Aid off now and be done with it, than to try the long-distance thing and find out down the line that it wasn't working. Maybe even after one or both of us had passed on a good opportunity in the name of fidelity.

She even threw the "we're both twenty-four and have our whole lives ahead of us" line at me. More numbers. More logic.

I'd thought that in those four months we'd found something special. Something worth fighting to keep.

Apparently I was alone in this.

Oh. That stream of numbers Abby hit me with. *Those* were definitely as cold as the falling snow. Colder even, maybe. After all, this was Portland, Oregon. We didn't get a whole lot of snow, and even if

the falling flakes looked tempted to stick around, the odds said they'd
be gone by noon tomorrow.

Odds were something I could focus on that would keep my attention off the colossal ache where my heart should have been.

I was standing at the bottom of the steps leading down from
Abby's apartment building. Gray skies of late afternoon overhead,
just starting to trend toward dusk. Stink of traffic in the air from all
the cars cutting down this "minor" street to avoid the "major traffic"
they'd hit a couple of blocks over on MLK.

They were playing the odds, of course. Probably all of them were
using an app to take the most "efficient" route possible. Because
saving a single minute in commute traffic, why, that could make all
the difference.

A minute a day, five days a week. Fifty weeks a year, allowing for
two-weeks off for personal time. Simple math said that could save a
whole four hours and ten minutes over the course of a year.

That was a lie, though. That minute a driver saves today doesn't
go into a bank to get stacked with all the other minutes saved driving.
Doesn't give that driver an extra four hours at the end of the year, to
spend hiking or reading or whatever.

A minute is still just a minute. And if, say, that driver has trouble
getting their mail out of their mailbox that day, that golden extra
minute is gone.

Okay. So maybe thinking about odds wasn't helping me. I had to
find something, though, or like a dark compass, my mind would keep
pointing to depressing thoughts.

Maybe I could find something beautiful to distract me?

All this snow, perhaps?

I studied the way the fresh fallen snow gleamed against the ... the
leafless – not lifeless, leafless – branches of the magnolia and
Japanese maple trees that skirted the sidewalk.

Normally, I would've found the sight pretty enough to give my
spirits a lift.

That day, though, the constant stream of cars, with their exhaust and their growling engines and their contrasting podcasts and music, that all played right into the heartbreak.

Hell, the exhaust fumes even ruined the taste of the last cup of coffee I'd ever share with Abby.

The world couldn't look beautiful right now. It was too busy looking ugly.

I wasn't dressed for snow because I'd figured on spending the night with Abby. Jeans and sneakers with a tee shirt seemed like a bad choice now. The jacket was heavy enough, and the Timbers scarf helped, but both were loose-weave wool and weren't designed to keep out moisture.

Ah, well. I could shiver for a couple of blocks and still be fine.

Question was, which way?

To my right, I could've walked two blocks to Rikki Tikki Tavern, where I could probably have run into a few of the guys, and drowned my sorrows in beer.

I couldn't face the guys, though. Not yet. I didn't want to tell them what happened. Listen to their takes, or their sympathy, or even anyone telling me I was better off.

Worst of all, if any of them started talking about "fish in the sea" or some cliché like that, I might say or do something I'd regret. Especially after a beer or two.

No. Instead, in this case, I'd have to play things Abby's way. I'd have to play the "smart odds" and just go home.

So I turned left. My own apartment was only one block down and one to the left, but in the falling snow it felt like a trek before I even started.

The sidewalks ahead of me already glistened a warning, ready to take me down if my attention slipped and I took too big a step. My sneakers were a few years old now, and their tread wasn't what it used to be.

Small, steady steps.

Other pedestrians passed me the opposite direction. I gave them as little attention as I could. Just enough to make sure I didn't walk into them. Which, to be honest, was more than a couple of them gave me. They were the sort who walked with their focus entirely in their phones.

I was around the corner and a block from home, the second time I barely avoided a collision with one such walking smartphone.

I caught myself thinking that I'd fallen so low I was less important than a small hunk of plastics and electronics.

Something snapped inside me.

Fire blazed out from my guts. I've heard it said that depression is anger turned inwards. If so, then a whole lot of inward-turned anger roared inside me. Instead of shivering in the cold, I felt feverish. Sweating, even. My heart surged back to life, beating hard enough that my adrenals woke up and got all my muscles twitching.

I spun, ready to tear that jerk's head off.

"Mew."

It was a tiny sound. A scared sound. The sort of thing that shouldn't have been able to cut through the haze of my anger.

But it did. That little sound. It was as though the wind had shifted, blowing snow in my face. Cooling my blood and smacking the anger right out of me.

That little sound didn't come from me, or from the jerk. I didn't know where it came from.

I stood there for a moment. Blinking. Frowning. Confused.

Alone. The jerk was gone by now.

I stood on cracked, uneven sidewalk, six houses from the little four-plex where I rented the back apartment.

I wasn't facing that direction, though. I was facing back toward Abby's street. A house to my right, where Oregon native plants in the vast front yard looked right at home under a comfortable – if thin – blanket of snow. The house was small. Postage-stamp, practically, in this neighborhood. Didn't look as though it had more than five rooms, and only a single floor.

Did have a lot of trees, though. A ring of six Douglas firs made that little house look like something out of a fairy tale. Where a witch would live, tucked away in the forest. Ready to help a traveler who played by the rules, or maybe to curse or eat the unwary ones, who didn't.

I didn't know the rules. And if a witch lived there, I didn't want to mess with—

Abby's street. A surge of sadness washed over me as I realized I'd reflexively referred to Olson Street as Abby's street. And that I'd probably think of it that way for quite a while.

My shoulders drooped. My head hung forward. I turned to slump my way back toward home.

"Mew."

This time I recognized the sound for what it was – the call of a frightened cat. Possible even a cat too scared to give full voice to its cry.

Came from my left. Somewhere among those Douglas firs...

There. A spot of orange among the apparently dead fronds of a fern that filled the area between two firs.

More than a spot, now that I could see it properly. And not really orange, either. More of a tawny color. And much too big for such a little cry. Even accounting for the *immense* amount of fluffy fur, this cat had to weigh a good thirty pounds.

How the heck had I not noticed such a big cat before?

Probably self-involvement and sadness.

I shook my head.

"Hey, there, little guy," I said, easing my way slowly toward the giant cat. "Or maybe you're a little girl. Can't tell from here, I'm afraid. But 'guy' can be generic, so if you don't mind, I'll stick to that for now. Not that you're all that little, you understand..."

I kept making that kind of nonsense talk, in as soothing a voice as I could manage, as I closed the distance between us. All the while, the cat watched me with curious eyes.

Curious orange eyes. Not yellow. Not green. But orange. I'd never seen eyes that color on a cat before. But then, I'd never seen a cat this big and fluffy before either. Biggest cat I'd ever met was a twenty-pound Maine Coon, and this one was much bigger.

Once I was within arm's reach, I held my hand out, nice and low.

The cat sniffed my hand a few times. Then looked at me again, as though considering me. Now, I hadn't known a lot of cats at that point in my life, but that seemed unusual behavior to me.

Still, the cat reached out and gave my hand a firm swipe with one cheek, which let me know I'd been accepted. I scritched the fur behind the cat's ears, and he pressed his head into the move and purred.

Oh, and what a purr. Louder than the traffic from Abby's – from Olson Street.

"You probably shouldn't be out in this weather," I said, as the cat came closer and twined himself – something about the cat's bearing seemed male – around my legs. Almost knocking me over in the process. "Let's go check with your people, all right?"

I crouched to brush a little snow from the wet outer layer of his fur, then hoisted the cat up to my shoulder.

Forty. That cat had to weigh forty pounds if he was an ounce. And I was pretty sure it was mostly muscle.

I carried him up to the house and rang the bell. An older, Korean lady opened the door.

"We don't want your cat," she said before I said anything at all. She started to close the door.

"Wait," I said, and was a little surprised when she did. Though I couldn't describe the look she gave me as *encouraging*. "So this isn't your cat?"

"We don't keep pets." She closed the door.

The cat leaned over and buffed my chin.

"All right," I said. "I like you too, but you're too big and healthy looking to not have someone, somewhere looking for you. So let's see about getting you home, all right?"

The cat, for his part, settled in against my shoulder and purred contentment. And I have to admit. As I carried that cat down the street to my Subaru Forester, I was smiling.

A FEW HOURS LATER, I STILL HAD THE CAT.

I'd taken him – and I knew for sure that he was a him now – to the vet, first. Alas, this cat had no microchip. Though the vet did confirm that the guy was in excellent health. And weighed closer to fifty pounds, than forty. Absolutely humungous for a housecat.

Gorgeous, too. Dried and brushed out, his fur was the color of dark honey.

The vet confirmed that he was of the Norwegian Forest Cat variety. Which just seemed like further confirmation that he was lost. Norwegian Forest Cats were rare in the United States, and an apparent purebred like this one couldn't just be a stray.

So the vet got the word out to all the local shelters, pet stores and pet hospitals about the big lug, and gave them my contact information.

Originally, the vet suggested I leave the cat with them, certain that the owner was likely frantic and would turn up within hours. But there were two reasons we didn't go with that plan.

The first was that the cat started yowling loudly and hissing at everyone if taken into a room without me, and would not calm down until I was allowed inside. The second reason was that, well, if the owner didn't show for some reason, I kind of liked the idea of adopting the cat.

I refused to name him until that time came, though. I was already feeling kind of attached to the guy, and naming him would only make losing him worse, when the owner showed up.

So I bought some cat food, toys, and a temporary cat litter – they make a disposable, travel kind of pan, it turned out – and brought the cat back to my place.

My apartment wasn't big by any stretch. One bedroom, and the living room split in two. The front half for the couch and television, and the back half for my desk and computer. What was supposed to be a little dining area served as my library, with Ikea shelves full of books around the walls. Though I did have a little, round kitchen-style table with two chairs, for when Abby... for when I had company.

The kitchen was a small, efficiency deal, but it did the trick.

I saw all this with new eyes as the cat wandered around. I told myself that he was just getting the lay of the land, but I swear he was studying me through studying my apartment. I thought I even spotted him tilting his head to read the titles of the books on my shelves.

The moment I caught myself wondering if he approved of my taste in fantasy and mystery novels, I shook myself and realized I had work to do.

I whipped out my phone and started posting to neighborhood apps, Craigslist local, and places like that. I didn't post a picture. I just described a found Norwegian Forest Cat – no mention of weight or color either – and asked the owner to contact me.

I didn't want some jerk trying to claim a cat who wasn't theirs just because they'd love a rare, purebred cat. Either to keep or sell. So I figured that whoever lost *this* cat would be able to tell me the color and weight.

I did take pictures, though, and print black-and-white flyers, which I posted around the neighborhood.

By midnight that night, I'd heard from four interested parties. None of whom knew what color the cat was. One came close, but got the weight and eye color wrong. Not even close.

I told every one of them that they should've been ashamed of themselves, trying to steal a cat.

I also got a lot of well-intentioned advice, suggesting I do things I'd already done.

By the time I went to bed that night, none of my efforts had gotten anywhere. At least, not as far as finding the cat's home. Still, I felt good that, while we searched, the poor thing wasn't huddled in the cold, hungry, lost and scared.

He was clean and warm, with a full belly and fur I'd brushed out myself.

When I went to bed that night, he jumped up onto the bed and curled up beside me, like a huge, rumbling teddy bear.

I woke with a start a few times that night. Not sure what I dreamed, but I'm pretty sure it was Abby-related. Probably stuff about heartbreaks, or loneliness, like dreams of ending up alone. Possibly as a crazy cat man.

Each time, though, the cat woke too. He gazed at me with heavy-lidded eyes, and purred me back to sleep.

Better than sleeping pills, that cat's purr.

When I woke in the morning, I felt a little bit better.

The cat wasn't there beside me, though…

I sat bolt upright, wondering for a moment if I'd dreamed the whole thing. But then I heard scratching from the temporary litter pan, and started laughing.

Calls about the cat began to taper off over the next couple of days. It seemed that even a small neighborhood had bigger matters to discuss than a single lost cat. There were coyotes to complain about, and noise, and all kinds of things people wanted to sell, or buy. Not to mention all the questions and opinions about various tradesmen, repair specialists and so forth. And the ongoing discussions about traffic, pedestrian safety, and complaints about the city council.

I called around to the shelters, pet stores and vets, but no one had come looking for a Norwegian Forest Cat. A fact that surprised them as much as it did me.

The harder part about the wait was that I was starting to get used to having the big guy around. He and I settled into a kind of routine. It was the weekend, so I slept in, mostly with him beside me. When I made my breakfast, I put out his and we ate together. I spent time on the internet, and reading, and watching movies – really, just trying to distract myself from thoughts of Abby – and the cat stayed nearby.

Sometimes even on my lap. And let me tell you. Having a fifty-odd pound cat on your lap disinclines you to get up. Feels like it wouldn't be worth the struggle.

Not that I thought he'd keep me there, if I needed to use the bathroom. He was quite observant, when it came to my needs and moods.

In fact, by the end of the weekend, I'd noticed that every time I'd started to dwell on Abby and heartbreak, the cat would entice me to play. I'd bought him a stick with a feather at the end of a string. And the cat was big enough that he could get to that toy anywhere I put it.

On top of the fridge? No problem. One jump onto the counter, one to the top of the fridge.

In a cabinet? No problem. He could hook one paw around the lip of the cabinet and pull it open.

No matter how clever I got at hiding that toy, all I had to do was sink into thoughts of Abby and suddenly there was a huge cat in front of me, feather toy in his mouth and stick trailing behind him.

Sometime over the weekend, I even found that I'd started talking to him. Oh, he didn't answer or anything, but I swear, he was listening. Whenever I talked to him, he was at least as good at paying attention as most of my friends.

When Monday morning came around and I had to head into work, I explained that to him. I told him about my job in cybersecurity for a local clothing firm, and when he could expect me back and such.

He didn't put up a fuss when I left, and he didn't knock over garbage cans or do anything else to express displeasure at my absence. When I got home, he was waiting with his feather toy in his mouth, ready for a game.

The week seemed to fly by. I called around to the shelters, pet stores and vets in the area twice each day, but nobody had come looking for a Norwegian Forest Cat. I updated my online threads, to keep them current, but the only calls I got were from people who hoped they could trick me into giving them a rare breed of cat that they couldn't begin to describe properly.

By Wednesday, I'd started to believe no one was coming for him. That maybe his previous people had moved out of state or something. That maybe he'd gotten lost during the move, or, worse, that they'd abandoned him.

Either way, on Thursday, I swung by the pet store on the way home and picked up more food, more litter, a few more toys, and an enclosed litter box.

He loved the food. He loved the toys. He seemed to love my big, cushy couch. I knew the cat had to have someone looking for him, but he just seemed so comfortable and happy, I'd started thinking of him as my cat.

I even named him. Behemoth. Just seemed to fit him, given his size. And Behemoth appeared to approve, purring at the prospect. Though, perhaps, the purr had more to do with the petting he was getting when I informed him.

I shouldn't have named him. I knew better. But I couldn't help myself.

Naturally, the next night Behemoth's proper owner came for him.

———

BEHEMOTH AND I WERE SITTING ON THE COUCH WATCHING TELEVISION. We'd properly shared a dinner for the first time that night. By which I mean I grilled some chicken on the stove, and gave Behemoth a share (in addition to his normal bowl of cat food).

Behemoth was curled up on my lap, but his eyes were open, as though he was paying as much attention to the television as I was. And he might've been. We were three episodes into an epic fantasy filled with magic, politics ... and cats.

The cats actually seemed to play a role in the story. They were all familiars, but they had their own goals, political issues and conflicts.

I was just resolving to find out if the show was based on a series of books when Behemoth's head came up, ears forward and attentive. He wasn't looking at the screen, though. He was looking back toward the front door.

"What's up, big guy?" I asked, but just as the question passed my lips, I heard a knock at the door. Three raps. Not loud, but firm.

Behemoth jumped down and started pawing at the floor, excited in a way that made my heart sink. I had the distinct feeling I was in for a second dumping within just over a week.

I forced a smile, though, and made my way over to the door.

I sucked in a breath, held it, and opened the door.

On my doorstep stood a woman who just did not look real. Real women couldn't possibly be that beautiful. Her long flowing hair didn't just look so silky that it invited touch, it was the color of sunshine glinting on gold. Her eyes, her skin, her figure – even dressed in a simple brown gown and adorned by nothing more than a necklace of amber, she was so dazzling that at a single glimpse, painters would break their brushes and give up their art, knowing that they could spend their lives attempting to convey such magnificence on canvas, only to inevitably fail.

The scent of her was warm mountain air, and honey, and something else enticing that I couldn't quite discern.

I don't know what happened to the breath I was holding. I don't even know how long I stood there, gawking like a teenager. But this incredible woman, she didn't seem to mind. Probably used to it. Got this kind of reaction everywhere she went.

I do know that what snapped me out of it was a *mew* of greeting from Behemoth. A very happy, full-throated sound.

"Please excuse me," I said quickly, clearing my throat. "I'm Lars, and I know you're not here for me. So I presume you're here for this little guy?"

As if on cue, Behemoth stepped forward and wound his way around her calves as though he'd done it a thousand times. An impulse that, I admit, I understood completely.

"I am," she said, "but I should like to come in, if you do not mind."

"Of course," I said, and she and the cat came in. Behemoth led her over to the small, round table in my library, where she took one of the two seats.

I closed the door and followed, struggling vainly not to watch her walk.

"Coffee?" I asked. "Tea?"

"Have you any wine or mead?"

I had to shake my head to focus on her words and not her voice. Her voice was every bit as beautiful as the rest of her.

"Uh," I said, and resisted slapping my own face at how ridiculous I sounded, "I don't have any mead, but I think I do have a pinot noir, if you'd like."

"Sounds lovely," she said, and I realized that she and Behemoth were looking into each other's eyes. He'd jumped up onto the table, and his whiskers and ears were moving as though he spoke to her in some kind of semaphore.

I opened the wine, and poured us each a glass. I left the bottle on the counter and brought the glasses. Set them down on the table, then took the other seat. All the while, she and Behemoth continued their intense eye contact.

I reached to pick up my glass, but she stilled my movement with her hand.

"Let it breathe," she said. "There's no reason to rush."

I frowned at that, for a moment. Certainly she might not have been in a hurry, but she couldn't know that *I* didn't have anything I needed to do that night.

Embarrassed as I am to admit this, though, not only did I not have anything better to do, the prospect of getting to spend a little more time in her company quickly set my heart racing.

I tried to tell myself, though, that it was just because I was thrilled that Behemoth hadn't left me yet. As though I could believe that. Given the physiological reactions I was having to this amazing woman, I couldn't even pretend they had anything to do with the cat.

Plus, I was girding myself to prepare for losing him. She'd already admitted he was her cat, and he certainly acted as though this were true.

By the time she looked away from Behemoth and at me, the wine was ready to drink. But she stilled my hand once more when I tried to raise my glass.

Darn it, I needed something to help with my strangely dry mouth...

She reached out with one hand and caressed Behemoth, who pressed against her hand and purred even louder for her than he did for me. A little detail that stole some of the shine from her beauty.

Behemoth was leaving me that night. And even though it was right and proper, it still felt like a second dumping. My stomach sank, and my heart lurched slower.

The woman frowned.

"You have had a rough time," she said, turning her amazing eyes on me again and stealing my breath. "Poor Lars. The pain of heartbreak is one of the worst in this world. But you have done me a great service." She stroked Behemoth's fur again. "You found this little one, when he got lost. You took him in and loved him as though he were your own, even though you strained to find the person he belonged to. He says only good things about you."

I didn't quite understand that last part, so I changed the subject. I had to clear my throat to speak. "So you saw one of the flyers, or...?"

"No," she said with a smile that warmed me despite myself. "I merely needed time to find him. But I'm afraid I cannot stay." She gave a small sigh. "Nor can I thank you the way I'd prefer to."

I was about to ask what she meant by that, but she reached forward and placed one hand over my glass of wine.

I have no idea what she said then. Or even what language she said it in. But the words. Her voice. They flowed out and around the room as though they had physical presence, and a warmth trailed in their wake. The lights dimmed as she spoke.

She withdrew her hand and smiled as though nothing strange had happened. The lights brightened again.

Behemoth must've felt the way I did, though, because he pawed the table excitedly.

"Shall we drink?" she asked. "Drain your glass. It's good luck."

I'd never heard that, but I wasn't sure I could refuse this woman anything.

We both drank down our wine. And mine spread a tingle all through my body. I could feel every inch of my skin responding. I swear I could even feel the tips of my hair, even though that's impossible.

She stood then, a single, graceful movement. "And now, alas, we must go."

"We?" I asked.

"Mjǫðr and I," she said, then reached out and stroked my cheek as though I were a cat, sending a thrill through my system that seemed to echo the tingle of a moment ago. "Though believe me. I would stay the night and thank you properly, if I could."

She and – Mjǫðr, I suppose – made their way to the door, and opened it.

"Farewell, Lars Alfson, and know that true love will find you before the change of the moon."

"Do I at least get to know your name?"

She smiled at me over one shoulder. "Well, I came as a stranger, and I did drink wine..."

Mjǫðr gave a sound of disagreement.

Her laugh made me shiver with pleasure.

"You're quite right, dear one," she said to the cat, "I've no need to contest his wisdom." She gave me a look of mischief and smiled. "Tell him my name."

"This night," the cat said, "you have hosted Freyja of the Vanir, and she has blessed you. Farewell, dear Lars."

———

If asked, I would never have guessed that I'd be able to sleep after finding out that I'd met and shared a drink with the Norse goddess of love.

And yet sleep I did. I didn't even cry my eyes out over the loss of Abby and Behemoth. In fact, when I woke the next day, I felt as though all of my sadness about both losses had abated to a place of calm acceptance.

I went to a shelter the next day to find a cat for myself, and came home with a cat and a date.

The cat was an orange tabby I named Whirlwind, for the way he never stopped moving.

The date was with Felicia, who would prove to be the love of my life.

THE BROKEN RULE

I used to have a cat who convinced me he could teleport. He was a huge, orange beast of a cat, and yet he had such stealth and speed that I could scarcely believe it.

I could see him, apparently fast asleep, in the living room. However, the moment I opened the right kitchen cabinet, there he was, slipping past me and into the cabinet before I could stop him.

Cabinets, closets, the refrigerator – no place was safe from him.

In fact, there were times I'd try to find him and couldn't. Huge freaking cat, but I could check all his hiding spots and see no sign of him. In an apartment small enough that there weren't *that* many places to hide.

No sign of the cat, though. Not until, suddenly, I'd realize he was standing beside me, wondering what we were looking at.

My wife and I used to ask him to teach us the secret of teleportation. He never did, of course. And the rationale I came up with to explain why he wouldn't, formed the basis for this story.

THE BROKEN RULE

I didn't rob those guys. I don't know who did, either. To be honest, I don't even know what was taken. What I do know is this.

It was a cold, rainy night in Portland, Oregon. Late October, when the cold is just getting noticeable, but the rain still feels refreshing after a hot, dry summer that ran overtime that year.

I'd been in Portland ... about two years at that point. A long time for me to stay much of anywhere, but the quirky nature of the city spoke to me. Told me things I didn't know I needed to know.

I actually kind of felt like I belonged in Portland. And when you've been as many places as I have, that's a feeling you never expect to get. Or at least, you don't expect to hold onto.

Everywhere a stranger. It's how I lived. Just ... my nature. At least, that was how I saw it.

I was leaving a brewpub in northwest, where the streets were just starting to slope on their way into the west hills. Buildings were packed in tight around there, apartments, houses and apartments side by side in a strange mix of zoning laws. Even some of the businesses still looked like more like old Victorian homes than stores.

"Painted ladies" an ex- of mine used to call those kinds of houses. I always liked that.

The brewpub was on the corner, and still rocking when I left. Noise level had gotten a bit much for me. The place was always a good kind of madhouse when the Timbers were playing an away game. Portland loved its soccer almost as much as it loved its beer. And anything that brought the two together was just this side of zeitgeist nirvana.

The Timbers didn't just win that night, either. They stomped down their hated rivals, the Seattle Sounders, in a key playoff matchup. Yeah, that pub was so noisy I could still hear the raucous celebrations going on half a block away.

I was smiling like a fool when I left. My spirits raised by victory and camaraderie, and my belly full of cheesy nachos and crisp IPA.

The rains were still fresh enough that I could smell them washing away car residue on the street beside me. Lots of cars out that night, but I was on foot and heading for the light rail station.

No need for me to drive to the pub when I lived two MAX stops away. I had my hood up, my jacket zipped up, and my shoes moving at a good clip down the sidewalk. Might not even be chilly by the time I reached the station.

First shouts I heard, I ignored. Figured they had nothing to do with me. They were coming from back down the block behind me, so I figured that maybe a couple of brewpub patrons had downed a few too many and needed to take out some excess energy on each other's faces.

Used to see that all the time around London. And while Portland supporters didn't have the ... exuberance of the English soccer hooligans, I still associated the sport with brawling fans.

But there was a moment of near silence. A moment when I was far enough away from the brewpub that the drone of rain muffled the celebrations. A moment when no cars were going up or down my block. A moment when the closest sound to draw my attention was shouted, loud and clear.

"That's the thief! Get him!"

I stopped and looked up. Figured I'd spot the thief. Maybe impede his escape, or at least notice where he ran.

But I didn't see anybody on the street ahead of me. Not for at least a couple of blocks. Not on my side of the street, or on the other side.

No bikes. No motorcycles. No other pedestrians.

I looked back down where I'd come from, figuring the thief hadn't reached me yet. That maybe that shout was meant to elicit my aid.

What I saw was not encouraging.

I did indeed see three men running down the street my direction.

Big guys.

Now, realize that when I say someone's big, that's coming from a guy who stands six-one and weighs close to two hundred. I'm a big guy. But these guys, they looked like they could bench press me, three reps of twenty each, and wouldn't need a spotter.

Not one of them had more hair on his scalp than a buzz cut, and only one of them – the one in the center – had a nose that didn't look like it'd been broken at least three times.

They weren't dressed for the rain either. Well, they heavy jeans and work boots, maybe, but they weren't wearing jackets. Just the kind of plaid flannel that seemed to be as close to a uniform as Portland had, for its guys.

They had the kind of bushy beards that completed the image.

All three of them glared at me while running, as though they intended serious bodily harm once they reached me. The one in the center gripped a combat knife with the kind of casual comfort that made me think he used to do bad, bad things in service to our country. And enjoyed it.

For a fraction of a second, I think I'd wondered if they'd just let me explain, or turn out my pockets and demonstrate my innocence. But the surge of adrenaline that jolted through my system suggested that explanations were best given in the company of the police.

And the likeliest place for me to find a cop just then? Near that light rail station.

"I didn't steal anything!"

I don't honestly remember deciding to yell that as I turned and ran. But I felt my lips form the words and heard the reverberations all though my head, so I knew they'd come from me.

Those nachos – and probably the beer – formed a knot in my guts before I'd covered two dozen paces. I pushed ahead anyway.

My eyes tracked back and forth, desperate for a uniform. Hell, any uniform. People respected firemen. And if I found an EMT, well, I might need one if the bulging trio didn't listen to reason.

Everything was brighter when I looked around. I mean, the streets downtown were pretty bright in the rain anyway. All the neon and sodium lights, reflecting off of all that fallen and falling water. But with my adrenals kicking into overdrive, my pupils must've gotten big enough to swallow all the light my brain could handle.

I was seeing so clearly through the downpour that if there'd been a cop, I'd've seen him.

I saw no cops. No security guards. No firemen. Not even an EMT.

I did see some people milling around a MAX car, either entering or leaving. Hell, maybe both. Not my place to judge.

The car was there. Which meant it'd be leaving any second.

I started cramping up. Not my legs. My guts. That belly full of food, coming back to haunt me.

I pushed through the forming cramp. Poured on a little more speed. Grateful that my sneakers were new enough that their tread could practically grip ice for me.

Didn't know how close my pursuers were. Couldn't risk a glance.

I lost a mental moment cursing the station's landscapers. Most of the stations downtown weren't all that different from bus stops. Spots at the curb to wait, maybe on a hard plastic bench under a rain shield.

This one, though, was at a corner. And the angle the tracks cut across, left them with a few dozen square feet for decoration. And damn them, they used it.

They lined the edges with hedges that came up to my waist. Added a thin Japanese maple every ten paces or so, with branches low enough that anyone jumping the hedge might hit their head.

Had to risk it.

Ducked as I jumped the hedge. The branch above me knocked

the hood back off my head. Ensured that my blond curls would soak before I could spare the attention to get that hood back up.

I came down on the other side of that jump at the edge of the grass.

My foot slipped on the grass. Started up into the air behind me.

Now, when you've done as much running as I have over the years, you learn not to let little things like that trip you up.

My foot took to the air behind me? Fine. I pushed off harder with the other foot and threw my hands forward into the dive, with my head tucked in tight.

I somersaulted across the tiny decorative cobblestones. My angle off just enough that my hips complained. Warned that I'd have bruises in the morning.

I just hoped those bruises were the worst I came away with from this.

Back to my feet and running again. The cramp in my guts getting stronger. Felt like it radiated from balls to collarbone.

A handful or so of people watched me with vague interest. Probably waiting for different trains than the one I was desperate to make. Not one of them looked inclined to get involved, much less help me.

Worse, I was pretty sure I heard a few big things plow right through those hedges behind me.

Not fair. Guys with that many muscles were not supposed to be fast runners. What, were they all ex-star halfbacks or something?

I had a lead on them, though. And I could hear the warning ping that the train was about to take off.

Odd, the thoughts that flit through your head in moments like that one. I realized that my pursuers had stopped yelling as they gave chase. So at least I was making them work. Might even take something out of their punches, if they caught me...

I leaned forward and poured on everything I had.

Man, I hoped no one moved into the nearest doorway. Even if I didn't run them over, I might vomit all over them.

I looked up just in time to see every door of that light rail train slide closed.

No.

No cops. No security guards. A handful of people, but I couldn't count on any of them helping. Portland was a friendly city, but only a fool would stand between those three and their prey.

And the nearest door to the MAX train was shut when I reached it.

But the train hadn't left just yet...

I could *hear* the boots of my pursuers. Not more than twenty feet behind me. Damn hedges must not've even slowed them down.

Now I admit. I could've turned to fight. Yeah, these guys were big. And yeah, they looked badass enough to work as extras in a show about motorcycle gangs. But with the kind of traveling I do, I'd done more than my share of fighting.

Except that there were three of them. One armed with a naked blade. And I was cramping up like those nachos wanted to come up and do the fighting for me. Staying here was a recipe for a beating or worse.

I saw only one good option. The option that had made me forever a stranger. The option that tempted me never to stay too long in any one place. It was the only way out of this mess that I could see, and I took it.

The doors to the MAX train were closed, but the train hadn't left just yet. The doorway was still there. So I reached to that doorway, and opened a Door.

The Door didn't exist until I reached for its handle. Then the Door shimmered into bright, golden presence as I pulled it open.

Didn't even look where it led me. Just slipped through and closed that Door behind me.

I was a kid when I first discovered Doors. Five, I think. Kindergarten age. I remember playing hide and seek at Derry Mulchester's birthday party. Derry's family had a huge house in

Portola Valley, California. Enough square footage to fit my parents' house two or three times, and still have room for the school library.

It was an old house, too. Lots of shadows and nooks, and warm, dark woods. Filled with the kinds of weird things that a history professor like Dr. Mulchester had accumulated over the years, from old globes to suits of armor to armoires and grandfather clocks and more.

Seems like an easy place to play hide and seek, right? Wrong. Derry's family held parties for the kids every month or so after the start of school. Every time they could find an excuse. So since it was almost Winter Break, all my classmates knew the best hiding places – and where to look.

Me, I was the new kid in town. Only been at the school since early December. So I was desperate to impress the other kids and maybe even make a friend or two at this party.

Thus I was frantic for the perfect hiding place. It was all I could think about. "Have to find the perfect hiding place. Have to find the perfect hiding place." I didn't think it in those words, you understand, but that was the focus of my entire being. The absolute devotion to a single concept that only a child can manage, and even then, only when properly motivated.

I could hear Trish Paulson's voice calling out from downstairs as she counted. She was at eight. She'd be starting after us at ten. And I still hadn't found a hiding place.

I reached for a door at the end of a hall. Looking back, I'm pretty sure it must've been Dr. and Dr. Mulchester's bedroom. But when that knob failed to yield to my pleading grip, I panicked.

I begged it to open. Begged it to give me a perfect hiding place.

There was a flash of gold, and the door came open. On the other side, just a little nook. Dark, but not pitch. Dim, like there were candles flickering nearby, but not in the alcove with me. It was warm and private, with only the one door, and a little davenport to duck behind.

I hopped behind that davenport. Hardly noticed when the door closed behind me. I just crouched down, smiling and hoping that I'd pulled it off. Certainly this couldn't have been a commonly used room. Smelled of must and disuse.

Time passed, and Trish never sounded any closer. I didn't hear the floorboards creak outside my hiding place. I didn't hear the sounds of anyone running for home base.

I didn't hear much of anything, really. My own breathing. My heartbeat.

Still, I was sure everything was fine. Why wouldn't it be? So I just settled into my hiding place, and entertained myself by savoring every last taste of that wonderful birthday cake that lingered among my teeth. The cake was a strawberry angel food, with strawberry buttercream frosting. Delicious.

But the cake only lasted so long. And the sugar had made me antsy, and thirsty. But I didn't want to be the dweeb who broke out of his hiding place early. So I gritted my teeth and dug in to wait.

Five-year-olds are not, in general, noted for their patience. But I was sick of being lonely, and felt certain that a good performance at hide and seek was all that stood between me and popularity.

So even when I was sure I'd waited as long as I could, I made myself count to a hundred before I'd come out of my hiding place. Then I did that two more times.

Finally, though, I was *sure* that Trish had to have found everyone else by now. Which meant that I could try to sneak back to the base and maybe even win. Plus, I was getting tired of hunching down behind a davenport that would've been much more comfortable to sit on, than behind.

I got up. Stomped feeling back into a foot that had gone to sleep. I strode to the door and opened it.

The hallway on the other side of that door was not one I'd come from. This one had ... some kind of weird looking, beige drywall. And the floor was a pale wood, with a runner fabric in patterns of red and yellow that made me think of movies my parents watched. Old ones, about kings and queens.

The hallway floor was also coated in dust. And the Mulchesters didn't allow dust in their home. I think it was against their religion.

Funny thing is, if I'd been an adult when this happened, I'd've walked out into the hall. Assumed I'd made some kind of mistake in my haste. Gone looking for the party.

As an adult, how could I possibly believe that I'd crossed over into some kind of other world?

But as a kid, it just made sense. I mean, I wasn't *expecting* it or anything. But I didn't question the evidence before me.

When I came into the little alcove with the davenport, I'd come from one hallway. But I was staring out of the same doorway, into a different hallway. No doubt. No question. Different.

Mind you, I didn't leap to the assumption that I was in another world. I just followed kid logic. I figured that the room had moved or something. Maybe it had spun. Or maybe it was a secret elevator, and it didn't have any buttons because it only went up or down, which-ever way it could go when the door closed.

Aha! The door was open. All I had to do was close it and...

Nothing.

When I opened the door again, the same dusty hall with the same weird drywall and rug.

Then I remembered the flash of gold.

I'll spare you the rest of my five-year-old thought processes. Point is, eventually I figured out that I'd wanted to find the perfect hiding place, and so I did. Clearly I had some kind of magic. I just needed to figure out how to use it.

Kid logic, yeah, but in this case it happened to be right.

Figuring out how to deliberately open a Door took a while, let me tell you. By the time I understood how I needed to think and focus to open a Door back to the Mulchester house, I was scared, half-starved and desperate for home. And food. And my parents.

Did impress the other kids though. Well, not as much as I would've if I hadn't come back shivering and, well, maybe crying a little.

All right. They were impressed. They just weren't *favorably* impressed. Especially since not one of them believed my story about Doors. And I couldn't seem to prove it.

See, I can only open one every so often. Takes me a good two hours to be able to do it again. And by the time I figured that out, I didn't care what the other kids thought.

I had magic, and they didn't.

THE DAY WHEN I WAS FLEEING FROM THE BULGING TRIO, I HADN'T HAD the time or focus to pick my destination. Not a great thing, but not dangerous in itself. See, I couldn't open a Door to anyplace immediately hazardous to me.

No risk of the vacuum of space, or the fires of a volcano or anything like that. If I put on a scuba suit first, I could open a door to someplace underwater. But only if I didn't try to go deep enough to risk problems with pressure.

No, I don't know what happens to the water I displace when I do that. I'm pretty sure it doesn't flow back through the Door though. Doors seem to be one-way.

Sometimes I opened Doors without destinations in mind just for the adventure of it. And since those efforts always brought me to some kind of adventure – I honestly did once rescue a princess from a dragon, for example – I figured there had to be some kind of subconscious selection going on when I opened a Door without a pre-chosen destination. Figured that explained the safety of doing it, and the tendency for me to find what I was looking for, even when I didn't know I was looking for it.

All those speculations melted away that day, like sugar in a rainstorm.

I came through that glowing, golden doorway sweaty, cramped, and panting for breath. My heart was pounding as though I were still sprinting for my life. My skin felt clammy, and those nachos were rebelling something fierce. Had to breathe slow and shallow to keep them from coming up.

Had my eyes closed, leaning forward with my hands on my knees. Not as dangerous as it might sound. I didn't feel a breeze, so I figured

I was inside someplace. Maybe even that alcove with the davenport. Though if so, it must've been cleaned since that first time, because I didn't smell the must and disuse. All I really smelled was, well, me. My sweat. The smell of nachos and IPA on my breath.

Once I managed to get my breathing and heartrate under control – and persuade those nachos to forget about coming up, I straightened and opened my eyes.

I stood on a road. Not dirt. Cobblestones in a rainbow of colors. Though it was a pretty muted rainbow. Narrow, too. Only maybe wide enough for my outstretched arms.

In and of itself, this was weird. A road, even a narrow one, could be dangerous. I didn't come through Doors onto roads. The side of a road, sure, but the middle? Unprecedented.

And that wasn't the only thing about this cobblestone road that was unprecedented.

There was nothing on either side of it. And I mean *nothing*. Blackness. I reached down to see if it was just darkness – which would've been odd, since I could see the road quite clearly, even though I didn't know where the light came from – and there was nothing to touch.

Something I hadn't realized until that moment – air has a sensation. We're just used to it. We live our lives in air, so unless the wind is strong or something else strange is going on, the casual presence of air isn't something worth noticing.

But I wasn't feeling air then, as I reached past the edge of the road. I could feel air against the skin of my face, my neck, my ears, my arm and so on. But my hand? My wrist, where it had reached over the side the road?

Nothing.

I frowned and waved my hand until I realized that what little I was feeling was the sensation of my nerves cried out for the familiar touch of air.

I pulled my hand back quickly, and shivered as the implications of what I'd felt – or rather what I *hadn't* felt – sank in.

No leaving the roadway. Got it. Must be why I came through here. It was the only safe place to stand.

But that didn't matter. I was here. I was safe. I checked over my shoulder, and sure enough, there was still a regular door right where I expected one to be. Looked to be made of cold iron, with supports riveted around the outer edge, and across the middle.

Wasn't much wider than the doors I was used to in modern Portland. It filled the road where it stood, though, because the road narrowed to the door's width.

Curiosity made me try the handle, but it was locked.

No, I did not try to lean out and look around. No way I was exposing my face to all that nothingness surrounding the road.

What I wanted to do was sit down and rest. Maybe even lie down. After all, I had some time to kill before I'd be able to open a Door again and go back to my apartment. Or wherever else felt intriguing, in case I decided to be done with Portland.

Sitting or lying down, though, would've been a mistake. After the intense – if moderately brief – bout of sprinting, sitting down to rest might bring on more cramps. Better to go walking. Maybe see what was at the other end of this road surrounded by nothing.

I'd come here, so maybe there was something here I needed. So I started forward to find out.

Hard to maintain visual perspective without a background for contrast, but it seemed to me that this road among the nothingness arched ahead of me. Which made at least some sense, given the muted rainbow pattern of the cobblestones.

Hey! Maybe there'd be a pot of gold at the other end. I couldn't recall ever actually looking for one of those. Didn't think the idea of finding a Door to the end of the rainbow had ever occurred to me.

Gave me something pleasant to speculate on as I walked.

I'd been marching up that arch for maybe five minutes when I spotted something ahead of me. And I don't mean a pot of gold. What I saw was small, and sat in the middle of the road in the distance. Didn't seem to be moving.

As I got closer, I could tell that it was gray and furry.

As I got closer still, I could tell it was a cat. Long-haired. Fur a pattern of darker dorsal grays and lighter ventral grays. Big, for a housecat. Maybe twenty or twenty-five pounds. Bright green eyes.

I stopped maybe thirty feet back from the cat. I mean, yeah, this *looked* like a cat, but I had no idea where I was. Given my history with Doors, I didn't expect the cat to be dangerous, but that didn't mean I should piss him off.

Piss *her* off?

No. The bridge of the nose was too wide for a girl cat. Most likely a boy.

"Hi," I said, trying several languages to be on the safe side. A habit I'd gotten into after running across a rhinoceros that spoke German.

No, I didn't know if the cat understood me. But I figured soothing tones were a good idea, even if the words didn't come across right.

I swear the cat seemed to frown at me. Just to be safe, I took that as comprehension.

"My name is Martin," I said. "What's yours?"

The cat's tail twitched back and forth. His ears folded back, then came up again. He rapidly washed a forepaw, then set it back down.

"You're not supposed to be here," he said, in English. His voice sounded young, strong and certain.

At least, if he were human, those characteristics would've applied. I'd never met a cat who spoke English before, so I wasn't sure how he was supposed to sound.

"I'm not? Where am I supposed to be?"

The cat gave a low sound of disapproval. At least, I hoped it was disapproval and not the start of a territorial challenge. I really didn't want to fight a cat. I loved cats. Had since I was a kid.

"I need to check your marks," the cat said. "Don't do anything stupid."

I frowned, and blinked in confusion as I tried to understand what was happening, but I nodded.

The cat strolled forward and circled me once, sniffing at my feet and ankles. When he finished he resumed his place in the center of the road ahead of me, perhaps ten feet away.

His tail whipped back and forth a few times. He washed his haunch, then used a forepaw to wash his face. He shook out his fur.

"You haven't been claimed in ... ten days?"

Ten days...

"The little Russian blue?" There was a small Russian blue cat in my apartment complex. He'd come to see me once in a while when I checked my mail, and I'd usually pet him. If any twigs were nearby, we'd play a bit.

And it was true, he usually scent-marked my ankles at least once when I saw him. But I hadn't seen him in over a week.

"And you don't know his name. So I presume you don't feed the Russian blue?"

"No," I said, frowning. I had to check myself from saying *he's not mine.* Implying ownership might not go over well. "He doesn't live with me."

The big gray cat leaned forward and gave his chest a few licks before sitting up again and regarding me.

"No cats live with you at all?"

"Not in a few years," I said. "I move around too much. Didn't think it'd be fair."

His tail twitched a few more times.

"No," he said, as though muttering to himself. "But someone must've shown him..." He stood, shaking out his fur. Louder, he said, "You're definitely not supposed to be here. How did you get here?"

I explained about Doors.

The answer didn't seem to please him. He must've done rapid washing for nearly thirty seconds before he resumed sitting.

"A cat lived with you in your kittenhood, yes?"

"Pollux," I said, answering without even thinking. "Flame point Siamese, and my best friend as a child."

"Pollux... Pollux..." the cat muttered a few times. "A flame point Siamese you called Pollux..."

His eyes widened and their green seemed to shine out like flashlights in the darkness. He said something else then, but it wasn't

English. If I heard it right, it seemed to be a combination of a meow, a yowl, and a purr.

"Uh," I said, raising my empty hands and backing away a few steps.

"Stop," the cat commanded, and my feet stopped moving before I thought to tell them to.

"Lower your chin," the cat said, again in that commanding tone. I had more control of my movements this time though, so I didn't move just yet.

"You're not going for my throat, are you?" I asked. A cat his size might just have claws wicked enough to pierce my jugular.

"Of course not," the cat said. "I need to check something. Now lower your chin to my level."

Problem was, if he was *going* to go for my throat, would he tell me?

"You know," I said, "I don't really need to know what's this direction. I'll just go back this way and wait until I can open a Door again."

I turned around.

The cat was right in front of me.

"Lower your chin for me," the cat said, "or you will never leave this road alive."

STARING AT THOSE BRIGHT GREEN, HEADLAMP EYES, I WONDERED IF I might've been safer back with the bulging trio. I mean, they weren't likely to outright murder me on the streets of Portland, in front of witnesses. They might only have put me in the hospital.

But this big gray cat. Something about him... I'd almost believe he could kill me if he wanted to. And that was a disturbing thought.

Not like I had anywhere to run from him, either. On either side of this muted rainbow of a cobblestone road seemed to be nothing at all – including air.

And I still had quite a while to wait until I could open another Door. Not that I had a doorframe nearby to work with.

"Last chance," the gray cat said. And maybe it was just me – or rather maybe it was just hope – but I thought he sounded sad. As though he didn't actually want to hurt me...

I swallowed hard, nodded, and lowered myself to all fours.

The cat came in close and sniffed my chin repeatedly.

I couldn't help smelling him while he was there. He smelled like sand and dry, desert wind. Reminded me of the day back in college when I went hiking in the Mojave with a couple of friends. They wanted to do it as a psychedelic trip on mushrooms. I was along to babysit.

The gray cat's tongue flicked out and lapped my chin once.

I burped then. Couldn't help it. The change in angle shifted the pressures in my belly. A waft of nachos and India pale ale, right in the poor cat's face.

His ears flattened, but he huffed a breathy chuckle as they came back up. He sat back on his haunches. Cocked his head at me.

"What do you call yourself?"

"My name's Martin," I said. "I didn't catch y—"

"Is Martin complete? Nothing else to it?"

I frowned at that as I sat back on my knees and feet. Not the most comfortable on those cobblestones, let me tell you, but I didn't want to bother standing in case the cat wanted another sniff.

Then the cat's words clicked.

"My full name is Martin Allen McDermott."

"Thank you," the cat said, which was unexpected enough that I had to catch myself on my hands or I'd've fallen forward.

The cat leaned back and yowled something to the nothingness above.

I wasn't sure what that was supposed to mean. Was it good? Bad? A death sentence? A reprieve? I almost asked, but the cat started washing his ears. I've been around enough cats over the years that I figured that was a delaying tactic.

So I waited.

A short time later, the strangest thing happened yet.

There was an answering sound. Like another cat yowling. Lower pitched than the gray in front of me. And anyway, he was still bathing when the sound started.

That answering yowl, it didn't sound as though it came from any distance. Not that distances were easy to judge, on an arching road surrounded by nothingness. Nevertheless, it sounded as though it came from close by.

I'd've said it came from behind the gray cat, but he looked up when the sound came, not behind himself.

"Where are we?" I asked.

"Somewhere you're not supposed to be," the cat said, absentmindedly. Still looking up, as though considering the answer he'd received. "But then, you're not supposed to be able to ... what was it you called it? Open Doors?"

The cat bathed himself a little more, clearly thinking, then finally gave his tail a flick and looked up at me.

"All right," he said. "The friend you called Pollux. How well do you remember him?"

"Very," I said, smiling at the reminiscence of that little flame-point ball of affection and mischief.

"Do you remember him surprising you, with the places you'd find him?"

"Yeah," I said, chuckling. "In fact, this one time he showed up on my bed, even though I'd swear I'd just heard him outside my window."

"Yes. Your bed. He slept there?"

"Yes," I said, smiling even wider now. Oh, how I missed that little guy. "The side of my bed was up against the wall, and he liked to curl up in this gap beside my pillow—"

"Showed up in your dreams sometimes, did he?"

I stopped smiling as I realized this gray cat was leading somewhere with his questions. "Yes. Still does, sometimes."

"That might explain it," the cat said, with a twitch of his whiskers that seemed like a nod.

"Explain what?"

"Why have you stopped sharing your home with cats?"

"You know how I got here?" I asked.

"Better than you do."

"Well, this power has made me a traveler all my life. And I didn't want to ever leave a cat behind."

"All right," the cat said, with another twitch of his whiskers. "I have decided."

"Decided what?" I had a cold feeling in my gut that maybe my lack of recent feline best friends might've targeted me for termination.

"Your ability to, as you say, open Doors. It is how your – and understand I mean no offense – more limited understanding of the universe allowed you to interpret feline teleportation."

"Feline teleportation?"

"There was a time when all cats could teleport. But we've been steadily losing that ability for some time now. Fewer and fewer of us can do it. Personally, I think befriending humans has made us too lazy."

"But—"

"Never mind the speculations," the cat said, which I thought was unfair, since he'd gotten to speculate. "The point is, against all edicts handed down from Bast herself, the one you call Pollux clearly taught you to do it."

"I don't remember—"

"You wouldn't," the gray cat said. "This sort of teaching would've been done in the dreamlands." His ears twitched as he looked me over. "You must be exceptional to have brought it forth with you into waking life."

"So what does this mean?"

"According to Bast's law, no human is to learn the ways of our tele-portation. So strictly speaking, I should not let you leave this road alive."

"But?" I said, hopeful smile in place.

"But the one you know as Pollux speaks well of you, as does the Russian blue who most recently marked you. Further, no cat will come forward to speak against you." His whiskers twitched. "And the damage has been done. So perhaps you should be given an opportunity to make things right."

"How?"

"You must do what you have not wanted to do. You must share your home with cats once more. And take those cats with you through Doors. That will remind them of what they've lost."

"I guess I can—"

"There is more," the cat said, so I let him finish. "You must find opportunities to take other cats through Doors as well. Not only the ones who share your home. As many as you can."

I crinkled my brow in thought. "I guess I could foster kittens. Show each of them while they're with me."

"Yes," the gray cat said. "That would be good."

"All right," I said. "I can agree to that."

"Excellent," the gray cat said. "But know this. I shall check up on you. And if you go back on your word, I shall steal your breath while you sleep."

"Well, that's adorable," I said, trying to cover the chill that passed through me then. "But not necessary."

"I hope it will not be. Goodbye, Martin Allen McDermott."

And just like that I was on a MAX car. Alone on a MAX car. That was pulling into the stop near my apartment.

The doors opened, and let me out into that cold, rainy October night.

My apartment wasn't going to let me keep cats. I'd have to move. Maybe it was time to get my own place. Either way, it looked as though I'd get to keep cats again.

But I'd have to find someplace else to watch Timbers games. If I was staying in Portland, I really didn't want to run across the bulging trio again.

I BLEED MUSIC

I keep a cat bed under my writing desk. Originally, I bought that cat bed for Dervish, who would get tired of waiting for me to finish writing for the day and come into my office and flop on the floor beside my chair.

Adding the cat bed made him more comfortable and had the side benefit of keeping his fuzzy self well out of the danger zone of my chair's casters.

Dervish, alas, passed a few years ago. And the cat bed had gone ignored by the other cats until little Khaavren came into our lives. He thinks it's a great way to hang out with me while I write.

Naturally, my wife and I started referring to him as my muse, or my writing familiar, depending on our mood.

The idea of cat as muse struck me the other day. But it couldn't be a cat living with someone. Otherwise I couldn't have much of a story, unless I put the cat in danger. Which I do not, as a rule, like to do in my stories.

I wondered where such a muse cat might live, and the result was this story.

I BLEED MUSIC

Twelve hours. Twelve hours I'd been a prisoner to my bandmates' farts.

This was no way to start a tour. Much less a tour that...

No. I wasn't going to start on that again.

We were riding in Fitz's van. At least, he called it a van. If you ask me, though, that thing might have come out of Dearborn as an Econoline, but it had been resurrected against its will so many times that I didn't think any proper car manufacturer would have recognized it as a vehicle.

Well, except maybe to pump a silver bullet through the poor thing's engine block and put it out of its misery.

Of course, there were those who might have tried to do the same thing to my band. God knows my parents wanted to.

You're twenty-five years old, Sinclair. Don't you think it's time you yadda yadda yadda...

My mom ran away from home at eighteen to join the Marines. Turned her back on decades of Pennsylvania blue blood to "do what was right for our country." Retired a full colonel after more than twenty years of service, and now she writes the Patriot Moms blog.

My dad didn't follow his parents into their pharmaceutical practice. He got really into Japanese flower arranging, in high school, and opened his own florist shop after getting a bachelor's in business.

Far as I was concerned, I was following my heart. Same as they did.

So every time they started yammering about responsibility and growing up, I tuned them out and thought about rhythm figures and melody lines. As I had since I was eight years old and picked up my first guitar.

A beat-to-death acoustic. An Ovation knock off that wouldn't hold a tune for more than for more than five minutes at a time. The frets and neck were in terrible shape, because some idiot had been putting steel strings on a guitar designed for nylon.

Paid five dollars for it at a garage sale. Probably more than it was worth, to be honest. But I didn't care. It felt right in my hands, and the notes that came out of it sent chills down my spine and smiles to my face.

I still have that old thing. Made a project out of fixing it up myself. Part of the reason I could give Fitz only so much shit about his van.

Point is, I bleed music. Until my parents understood that, they wouldn't understand the rest of it.

And they sure wouldn't understand why I would take time off my day job to drive up the coast in a trashed van with three other guys who smelled like they'd had nothing to eat but chili for the past week. All to play five gigs over ten days, in five different cities across two states. None of this anywhere near San Jose, California, where I lived, save that they were on the same coast.

And while I'd never agree with my parents about giving up my music, if they'd come at me about the tour right then, I might've conceded the point. Especially since...

No. I'd gotten over that. It was just the ride getting to me.

Twelve hours in this van's "backseat" might've driven Sid Vicious himself to put on a suit and get a desk job.

When Ford originally built this van, decades ago, they gave it two seats up front, with nothing but cargo space behind them. To "accommodate" our four-man band, Backmasking, Fitz had bolted a bench seat behind the original seats, just far enough back for a pretense of leg room.

Fitz claimed he'd salvaged that bench seat from some kind of bigger-than-big SUV.

I didn't buy it. Too small. Thinly padded. Covered in cheap vinyl. I figured that bench seat was much more likely to have been ripped out of some variety of economy car.

Worst of all, that vinyl both looked and smelled as though it had been dipped in bleach.

I always tried not to think about why someone would use that much bleach on a car's bench seat. But every time I strapped in, I couldn't help pondering what bodily effluvia had been "purged" from the thing I sat on. Made me consider bungee-cording myself into the back, with our gear.

I was sitting on that bench seat then, though. With Royce, our drummer, fast asleep beside me. I'd wedged his khaki duffle bag between us, to keep him from rolling over onto me and drenching my 69 Eyes tee shirt in his drool.

It had happened before. Behind his kit, Royce was two hundred pounds of bald Nubian hellcat. But fast asleep, the man was a damned waterfall.

Speaking of waterfalls, I was pretty sure we'd been driving through one since about the time we crossed the Oregon state border. I mean, no place could rain this hard, this long. Could it?

It was freaking April. I'd always thought that April showers May flowers thing was a myth.

But that rain just kept pounding on the roof. And sooner or later, that roof would give out. I was sure of it. I mean, everything else in the van had, at one point or another.

The only question was when.

Not something I wanted to be thinking about. Especially not when I was cold, tired, hungry, and sick to freaking death of the way these guys seemed to pass gas as though it were some kind of ongoing olfactory argument.

So, naturally, this was when Fitz said, "Uh, oh."

Royce snorted, like he might wake up, but rolled over and went back to dehydrating himself.

From the shotgun seat I heard Emilio start a whispered conversation with Fitz.

Oh, no. They weren't leaving me out of this.

"Uh, oh, *what*?" I said, nice and loud.

"Well," Fitz said, as I realized we were slowing down, and I could hear that he'd put on the turn signal. "Uh, oh, as in the van's done for now."

"What do you mean 'done,' Fitz?" I knew how dangerous I sounded, and I wasn't the least bit sorry.

"Not sure yet," he said, trying to placate me with his tone, if not his words. "Might be an overheating issue. Maybe baby just needs a little rest."

I didn't grace that with a reply. We both knew the van wasn't overheating in this cold, rainy weather.

"Stay chill, Sin Man," Emilio said. "We got this."

Emilio. Always our peacemaker. Easy smile, even while playing a fearsome bass guitar, but the kind of muscles and tattoos that made sure no one picked on him for being short.

Fitz was our carrot-topped lead guitarist. Skinny as a mic stand, but tenacious as a bulldog. And a damned virtuoso on the fretboard. Which was the main reason I put up with his shit.

Well, that and the fact that we'd been best friends since we could walk.

Which, let's be honest, was part of the reason he put up with my shit, too. After all, I didn't just play rhythm guitar and keys. I also sang lead. And nobody does that without at least a touch of arrogance.

Or narcissism. Depending on who you ask. And when.

The van rolled to a stop. The turn signal kept going. Which meant it wasn't the turn signal. He'd hit the flashers. Which Fitz wouldn't do if he just planned to sit while the engine cooled down.

"Fitz," I started, but Emilio gave me the chill-out signal and pointed to himself. Lighting was pretty dim, but I realized he had his phone to his ear.

I bit the inside of my cheek, and listened while Emilio called for a tow. He spoke quietly, which meant I had to almost strain my ears to hear him over the pounding rainfall. But I got at least part of it.

If I heard him right, the stupid van had sprung an oil leak.

What I didn't like – apart from the obvious – was that the conversation Emilio had with the dispatcher sounded more involved than, "oil leak, send tow."

Which meant they were trying to hide something from me.

***

FAR AS I WAS CONCERNED, I SHOULD'VE BEEN NOMINATED FOR DAMNED sainthood, all the patience I displayed that night.

Ninety-minute wait for the tow truck driver to grace us with his presence?

Ol' Sin Man kept his cool.

Getting towed twenty miles *farther* from our first intended stop to a town so small they called it Littleside?

Just call me Frosty.

Finding out that the only service station in town wouldn't even *open* until noon the next day, because the owner was up in Newport on a family matter?

Just rolled off my back like sleep-drool off Royce's shoulder.

But then I found out that there were no cheap, chain motels in Littleside. No proper motels at all, in fact. Sucked to be us, but I was figured that meant a night crashing in the van. We'd done it before.

Oh, no. Not in precious Littleside, Oregon. No, the sheriff – because apparently Littleside didn't rate its own police force and had to rely on the county for law enforcement – was informed of all dispatch tows, and would be checking to make sure no one slept in our van.

If we did, we'd face a misdemeanor charge worth a five hundred dollar fine and two nights in jail. Each.

One might ask why the penalty was so steep. Certainly I did.

According to Devon the tow truck driver, it was to discourage wandering college students from using the jail as a free night's lodging on their way up and down the coast. Which was a thing. I guess.

My next choice, of course, would've been to just pick the nearest twenty-four-hour restaurant and wait out the night there.

I didn't even bother asking. One glance up and down the main road – which also happened to be Highway 101 – made it clear that this was not a town that had twenty-four-hour anything.

Devon dropped us off outside our only real option. The Little Night's Sleep, a freaking bed and breakfast. I'm sure that, by sunny daylight, it probably looked cute and quaint. A darling little house perched near the cliff's edge to have wonderful ocean views.

But it wasn't bright, cheerful daylight. It was a goddamn freezing night, with what had to be the whole planet's rain allotment coming down on our heads.

I was soaked to the marrow, and would've sworn I'd been dropped off at Norman Bates' house. All evil angles and threatening windows. Trees and bushes whipping back and forth like they wanted to grab us and fling us into the Pacific.

And that, my friends, is when my patience reached its end.

Fury blazed heat and power through my system.

"This is all your fault!" I bellowed at Fitz as I lunged for him.

Emilio, brilliant peacekeeping Emilio, must've seen it coming. He'd positioned himself and Royce in just the right spots to catch me when I went for Fitz. Between them they had enough muscles to punch through concrete.

But me, I was quick and wily. And all three of us were sopping wet. I slipped right past them.

Fitz was already running around those whipping trees. Fast on his feet, the skinny Irish fucker.

Emilio caught me then. Not sure how he managed it. But he grabbed me from behind, gripping his other wrist with fingers strengthened by years of playing the bass.

I kept yelling anyway.

And I started with the one thing I'd been trying not to think about on the whole twelve-hour drive up here.

"*Denmark*, you said! You found us a gig in *Denmark!*"

"It's a city in Oregon!" Fitz said for what had to be the hundredth time since he'd first booked the gig.

I writhed in Emilio's arms, but though we were both *soaked* I still couldn't get free from his iron grip. And even furious as I was, I wasn't stupid enough to try elbowing Emilio's face. This was a man who could heft me over his head and throw me.

So I kept at Fitz verbally.

"Funny you didn't mention that part until after we'd all put in for time off."

"Yeah," Royce said. "I even updated my passport."

"No," Emilio said. "Not you too. Enough!"

He swept my legs and dumped me on the gravel hard enough to stun me for a moment, then sat on my chest. My heart lurched from pounding speed metal time to the slow, heavy opening of Sabbath's classic "Iron Man."

"Sin Man," he said, while I remembered how to breathe, "I agree it's fucked up that he held back that the gig was in Oregon, not Europe. But a gig is a gig, and we need to expand our fanbase."

I wanted to argue, but it was difficult with rain pouring down on my face and a bass player on my chest. Plus, that whole breathing thing wasn't too easy, the way Emilio compressing my ribs.

Worse, he kept talking, in that peacemaker tone of his.

"Besides. You know what? That little deception gave us an excuse to come tour. Actually tour. Get some road legs, instead of playing the same old clubs. And yeah, maybe his van broke down, but do *you* have a vehicle we could've used?"

I gritted my teeth in defiance.

"Do you?"

Eyes still trying to stare pain at him, I shook my head.

"What about you, Royce?"

"You know I don't."

"Damn straight. Now. If you promise to stop stressing your voice, Mr. Lead Singer, I'm going to let you up. And then we can all go inside and get *dry*. And *warm*. Doesn't that sound better than fighting in the rain?"

Not gonna lie. I was still mad enough to snap Fitz like a guitar string. Too many hours suffering in that van, only to have the fucking thing break down. Again. On top of everything else, calm was just not an option.

And if Emilio was counting on a face full of rain to help cool me down, he missed on that one. Just pissed me off all the more that Fitz's van had dumped us here, of all places.

Yes, I understood the logic of everything Emilio was saying. But right then, I was a creature of pure emotion. And none of what I was feeling could be construed in a positive way.

Still, I gave him a terse nod – if nothing else, I wanted to get up.

Emilio studied me like he could read my thoughts. Grimaced and shook his head.

"Royce. Fitz. You guys go get us two rooms. When you have the keys, Royce, bring me one. I'm going to keep Mr. Attitude here on the front porch until then."

I heard the front door slam shut before Emilio was willing to let me up off the gravel.

True to his word, he at least got me out of the worst of the rain and up onto a wide wooden porch that had a two-seat rocking chair and a round stone painted with a sunflower and the word "welcome" on it. Emilio even had the decency to stand there shivering beside me while we waited.

The smell of rain and sea should've been a pleasant change from all those farts. But just then, it smelled like mildew and decay.

When the door finally opened, Emilio took the key from Royce, but didn't let him come outside.

"All right," Emilio said, turning to me and holding up that key. It wasn't a keycard, but an old fashioned looking brass key. "This is how it's going to go. You're getting your own room tonight. It's not a favor.

It's solitary confinement. And you need to use that time to figure your shit out and get over the Denmark thing."

Eyes narrowed, I started to object, but Emilio held up a hand for silence.

"I mean it. We've put up with your stewing on the whole drive up here, but we're not doing ten days with it. Not even for your killer voice and songwriting chops. So do whatever you need to do to put this shit behind you. And when I see you at breakfast in the morning, I expect to see the charismatic motherfucker who got me to join this band. The one who makes nightclubs rock and panties drop. You still that guy?"

I nodded.

"Say it."

I was shivering so hard I needed three breaths to get the words out without stuttering.

"I'm the guy who makes nightclubs rock and panties drop."

"I don't believe you," Emilio said, shaking his head. "By the morning, I'd better."

He gave me the key then, and turned and went inside.

Did our *peacemaker* just threaten to have me kicked out of my own band? The band that had been my idea in the first place, back when Fitz and I were...

Great. Just one more thing pissing me off.

If the room didn't have a heater, I'd warm up by setting fire to the place.

It had a heater. Food too. A bread and cheese plate that I wolfed down so fast I wasn't sure afterwards if the cheese had been cheddar or gouda. Pretty sure the bread was rye.

The room even had a bathroom with its own shower, and I probably used up every bit of the hot water drumming feeling back into my numb extremities.

Unfortunately, even a good shower wasn't enough to calm me down. Especially since the room was so *very* pink...

The floor was some pale hardwood, but most of it was covered with soft, pink rugs. The walls were painted a soft shade ... of pink. The queen-size bed? Pink bedspread over red sheets, with pink pillowcases.

Two windows looked out over the raging Pacific. Their sills were a darker shade of pink than the walls. But their curtains matched the walls.

The bureau and twin nightstands? White with pink trim. The *lamps* on those nightstands? Pink lampshades. Matching the one covering the ceiling lamp.

Hell, even the smell of the room was pink. I swear, it was some kind of potpourri of posies and roses.

I felt like I'd checked into Barbie's Fucking Dream House. Even the wall decorations were paintings on the walls of kittens at play. If I hadn't immediately dropped my duffel and stripped off to shower, I'd've had to check to make sure no one had given me the Ken doll down there.

Have to admit, though. The heater did work. Pinged and knocked, but it kicked out enough hot air to keep me from freezing to death.

So I didn't *have* to set fire to the place.

Jury was still out on whether or not I would.

I mean, I'd never burned a place down before, but mad as I was that night...

Bad enough I was stuck in Littleside, Oregon, which might as well have been the thirteenth century, far as any late-night amenities went.

Bad enough we couldn't just crash in the van overnight. No. We had to drop the cash to sleep in a *bed and breakfast*. Where the rooms were clearly designed by someone's seven-year-old daughter.

Bad enough about the Denmark thing. Getting my hopes up like that. Fitz knew I'd always wanted to tour Europe.

Bad enough about the van breaking down again, and Emilio talking like he's ready to kick me out of my own band.

All those things were bad. But worse than any of them?

I was so pissed at Fitz that I'd forgotten to ask Emilio what *else* was wrong with the van. Because I knew it was more than an oil leak. Now I had all night to stew about that too. Because if the tranny was shot – or anything along those lines – we were D.O.A. There went any chance of our making the Denmark, *Oregon*, gig, and probably not the Eugene gig either.

Hell, in a two-bit town like this one, that might mean the end of the tour right there.

Heater must've been working overtime, because thinking about this stuff got my skin downright feverish. Even though I was wearing nothing but a towel while pacing back and forth on the pink carpets.

My fists were forming balls on their own, so I stopped and forced them to unclench. I needed to go back into the bathroom and comb out my hair while it was still wet. I kept it short these days, but it still looked better combed than not. And the routine might help.

It didn't. Neither did hanging my soaked clothing on the shower rod to dry out.

The room came with a bathrobe that was white, at least, so I put it on and went back into the bedroom to figure out what I was going to do.

Well, that was the plan. Unfortunately, that fell by the wayside, because combing out my hair had given me enough mental space to find something more to get upset about.

An ultimatum. Emilio the Peacemaker had given me an ultimatum.

Me!

Backmasking was *my* band. My idea. My songs. My voice. If anyone was going to give ultimatums around here, it was *me*.

I was wearing a path in the pink rugs and fuming about the series of injustices that had led to my captivity in this pink, pink room during a rainstorm on the Oregon coast, when something caught my eye.

A spot of orange among all the pink.

In the center of the bed.

An orange tomcat lounged there, staring at me with yellow eyes. I glanced around, but the door to my room was still closed, and I hadn't heard it open. And obviously all my windows were closed, or the winds and rains would more than overpower the heater.

I looked back at the cat, who regarded me lazily. Purring, just loud enough for me to hear him. There was no question that he belonged here. His collar was pink. Even had a little seashell in the front that named him Puffer.

"Puffer, huh?" I said, looking him over. He had short fur, but almost tiger-striped by darker shades of orange over lighter shades, with a belly that was lighter still. Almost cream in tone. One of his ears – the right one – had been notched pretty good. Legacy of some old fight, probably.

"If you're hoping to puff some weed," I said, "you're in the wrong room. I don't smoke. And I mean anything."

The cat sniffed at the air.

I started laughing. I swear, it felt like the cat was trying to scent-check my honesty. Like he expected to smell pot or something, and was ready to unleash a judgmental meow if he detected it.

"Judgmental Meow." Might make a good song title. I had an ex-, Clarice, who was this gorgeous redheaded dancer. She had a big gray tom who hated how much attention Clarice gave me. Got to the point that when her hands were on me instead of him, he started letting out this loud, territorial yowl.

I grabbed my songwriting notebook out of my duffel and sat down on the bed to take a few quick notes toward a song called "Judgmental Meow."

But a few quick notes became a chorus. And verses. Then I was writing down chord progressions and jotting down the melody line and...

Next thing I knew, I didn't just have one new song. I had two.

The other one, "Fire Dancer" was about Clarice. She wasn't a literal fire dancer, she was a ballerina. But when she got twirling, that red hair of hers looked like flames, and the rest just sort of flowed outward from there.

When I came up for air, I turned to say something to the cat. But the moment I saw those yellow eyes, I remembered the way Clarice used to look at me sometimes, when we were alone late at night. She'd drape her hair in front of her face, and the look in her eyes would get positively feral. Like a stalking tigress.

And oh, how I loved it when she pounced.

I called that one "Tiger Eyes," about the thrill of being stalked in a good way. But no sooner did I finish that one then I remembered the fight that led to the end of things between me and Clarice.

She hated that I sang lead. Hated that I was the front man, getting all the attention. Even though she was my girlfriend – and no, I never cheated on her or any other girlfriend – she felt like she was in competition with every other woman in the club, each time we performed.

I tried telling her that there was no competition. For me there was only her. Alas, the more I tried explaining that she was worrying over nothing, the more worried she got.

Finally she asked me to give up singing lead, for her. To find another lead singer, and settle for playing rhythm guitar and keys. Maybe singing backup.

I asked how she'd feel if I asked her to never dance another solo.

She didn't see it as the same thing at all. And once the yelling started, that was pretty much the end of our relationship.

All of that and how I felt about it came pouring out into a song I called "When the Yelling Starts."

As I finished that song, I thought about the yelling I'd been doing earlier. But I wasn't ready to think about that. So instead I thought about Maria, another ex- who'd dumped me even though things were going great.

It seems her mother had told her: "you like someone because, but you love someone in spite of." And though Maria could think of a bunch of things she liked about me, she claimed she couldn't think of any in-spite-ofs. Which meant she only liked me. That she didn't love me.

Ridiculous. I know. Especially since it made me sound as though I didn't have faults, which I more than obviously did. I mean, that night in Littleside alone was more than enough proof. Hell, Fitz and I had more than our share of "in spite ofs" about each other. And I could think of a few about Royce and Emilio, and I had no doubt they could about me.

Still, thinking about Maria led to a song called "I Like You Too Much to Love You," which was like a catalog of my faults, as viewed by girls who either liked them or hated them.

When I finished that song, I wondered how many faults I could name that my bandmates would list...

That song I called "Warning Label." As in the things prospective bandmates should know about me before signing on. Really, it was also a warning about lead singers in general. And it led on into another song about Fitz and me called "Our Blood Is Music."

Fitz was the one who first said that about me. That I bleed music. He said it when we were ten. I'd broken a string on that old Ovation knock-off, and the broken string cut my hand. Fitz, who was standing next to me playing his own cheap acoustic, said he was shocked that blood came out of the wound, not music.

I said that if I bled music, then so did he.

That was how my night went in that pink, pink room. Every song seemed to lead right into another. And if it didn't, I just had to look at Puffer and some memory would trip and I'd be off and writing again.

I didn't even get under the covers that night. I fell asleep with my pen in my hand.

ROYCE IS BIG ON "ACTIVE DREAMING" OR "LUCID DREAMING" OR WHATEVER he was calling it at the time. The name changed periodically, depending on what he'd most recently been reading, but he credited it with some of his best drum work. Claimed he practiced in his dreams, and came up with things that made other drummers break their sticks out of jealousy.

Me, though, I didn't usually remember my dreams. Most I

normally got was some kind of vague emotion. Like a good dream or a scary dream. That kind of thing.

But when I woke up that next morning in the pink, pink room, I remembered some of what I was dreaming about.

And all of it was about Puffer.

Puffer and me, walking through a forest of huge coniferous trees. Puffer and me, strolling along a gray shoreline where we had to watch out for sneaker waves. Puffer and me, sitting on a rock and staring out over the ocean at sunset. Him on my lap, purring, while I stroked his soft fur.

When I woke up – facedown on the comforter with pen in hand and still wearing that white robe – I felt peaceful. For maybe the first time since Fitz had mentioned the detail of our Denmark gig being in Oregon.

The colors of the room, the smell of the posies, none of the things that drove me crazy the night before seemed to bother me that morning.

I didn't even feel stiff or sore when I sat up, laughing about the mix-up for the first time. I mean, that Emilio, Royce and I were expecting Europe and got Oregon. And as I laughed, another song came flowing out of me. "Denmark Rocks, Part 1."

Had to be part one, because I'd write part two after we played the gig.

I got dressed in torn jeans and a Misfits tee, got my stuff together, and looked around for Puffer, to say goodbye.

Cat must've gone back into hiding. Wherever he'd been when I first came in. I didn't find him under the bed, in the closet, or under any of the furniture. But one thing I knew for sure about cats – they could find hiding places we'd never think of.

So I shrugged and stopped looking.

I was ravenous for breakfast. Still. I couldn't leave without saying something to Puffer.

I couldn't quite explain it, but as I'd gotten dressed a few minutes earlier, I'd found myself thinking about the songs I'd written the night before. And about the way that just looking at Puffer always seemed to trigger another.

I had to give the little guy his due before I left.

"Bye, Puffer," I said, addressing the room with a quirked little smile. "Thanks for helping me get my head on straight."

I turned to leave the room then, and stopped dead with a chill running down my spine.

Right beside the door. A painting of kittens at play. One of those kittens, a tiger stripe tom with a notched right ear...

I started laughing. Ridiculous. All the pink in the room had to be getting to me. Obviously someone had commissioned the painting from a local artist, and asked to have the bed and breakfast cat included in the work.

Heck, for all I knew, each of the five kittens in the painting was a full grown cat, somewhere in the building.

Addressing the painting this time, I clicked my heels, gave a stiff, formal bow, and said, "Farewell, Puffer. May you always have friends to play with, good food to eat, and a comfortable lap waiting when you want to sleep."

With that, I went downstairs to find my bandmates and breakfast.

The dining room was right at the bottom of the stairs. Quaint and charming as, no doubt, the whole place was when viewed by someone who wasn't cold, wet, tired and angry.

The hardwood floor had wide slats of a warm, orangey wood. The table had been whitewashed, and so had the eight chairs. The chairs had pale blue pads decorated with flowers, which matched the tablecloth.

Even had lace doilies under the white, stoneware plates and cups. I mean, this place had everything.

Everything except food, so far, that was. I could smell eggs and bacon cooking, but the smell was coming through a door into what had to be the kitchen, not from the plates on the table, which were empty so far.

Everything did, however, include my bandmates. I'd heard their voices while coming down the stairs, but they'd stopped talking when I came into the dining room.

All three of them looked up at me. Fitz, grimacing, ready for a harsh word. Emilio, suspicious, and possibly ready to leap into action. Royce just looked like he wanted to get this over with, one way or the other.

I dropped my duffel bag and broke into a big smile.

"Twenty," I said. I held up my notebook. "I wrote *twenty* songs last night. Not just lyrics, either. Music too. Full notation."

Whatever they were expecting me to say, that wasn't it. All three of their jaws dropped. Twenty was the kind of output that usually took me at least two or three weeks.

Fitz was the first to start smiling.

"Uh, Sin Man," Emilio started, still as wary as Royce, but it was my turn to hold up a hand for silence.

"I know," I said. "I owe you all an apology. I've been—"

"Forget it," Fitz said, giving me that lopsided smile that told louder than anything else could have that he and I were okay.

Just when I'd thought I couldn't feel any better.

"No," Emilio said, "I want to hear this. What are you apologizing for, Sin Man?"

"For being a prick to deal with lately. For getting physical about it last night, at the worst possible time. For holding onto anger about the Denmark thing, instead of getting excited to play new venues for new fans. And for acting as though it was all an affront to me, personally, instead of a communication breakdown."

Fitz mimed playing guitar and sang the first few bars of the guitar opening for Led Zeppelin's "Communication Breakdown."

I started laughing, and all three of them laughed with me. I grabbed an empty chair.

"I was thinking," I said. "We should have some time to kill before the van's ready. Eugene's our second stop, right?"

"Yeah," Fitz said. "The Bass Note, on University."

"Exactly," I said, thumping the table. "A college town. Maybe we can make some calls this morning. Get some interest from their college radio station."

"Who are you and what have you done with the Sin Man?" Royce asked, chuckling at the thought of me, coming up with marketing ideas for the band. That was usually his role.

Emilio chuckled, shaking his head as though the laugh was against his will. "That's him, all right. That's the man who got me to quit the Caballeros to play with you guys in the first place."

Emilio reached across the table to give me an exploding fist bump.

"We ... may have more time for phone calls than we want," Fitz said, grimacing as though he were afraid to ruin all the good will. "I was seeing signs of wear from the clutch last night, too."

Still smiling, I shrugged. "So we call around about a clutch, and maybe we don't roll into Denmark until close to showtime. We'll still hit the ground ready to raise hell, won't we?"

That got me a round of hell-yeses, perfectly timed for our breakfast to come in.

The woman carrying our breakfast on a big, silver tray was pretty enough that I gave her the full-wattage smile. She had chestnut brown hair tied back in a ponytail, and a blue and yellow dress that had to have been thrilled to be worn by someone like her.

Yeah, she was twice my age and married, but I wasn't trying to start anything. I was just feeling good and wanting to share. Thus, the smile.

Had the effect I wanted, too. Got her smiling back, even as she was shaking her head.

"Coffee'll be out in a minute," she said as she distributed plates of bacon, eggs and very fluffy pancakes. "We've got maple and blueberry syrup for the pancakes. If there's anything else you need, just let me know."

"Excuse me," I said.

"Yes, I have a sister, but she's married too," she said, smiling, with one eyebrow raised. "And I wouldn't let my daughter anywhere near you."

"Good call," Fitz said, while the other three of us chuckled.

"Not that," I said. "I was wondering if all the rooms come with cats, or just the pink room."

"Pink room?" Fitz asked, but I gave him the hand-wave that he'd know would mean "tell you later."

"Cats," she said, with more wonder in her voice than I expected. "What cat did you see?"

"Orange tom, with a seashell collar naming him Puffer."

Her eyebrows shot up. "Really?"

"Yeah," I said, more and more confused now. "He hung out with me all night, pretty much."

"You're the songwriter of the group?"

"Well, we all contribute," Royce started, but Emilio spoke over him. "He's the primary songwriter, yeah."

She nodded. "Consider yourself lucky. Puffer doesn't show his face for many, and if he hung around that long." She gave a breathless chuckle and shook her head in wonder. "You must've had some night. Hope you got all those ideas down. And I hope you thanked him."

Fitz started to make a joke but I waved him to silence and kept my eyes on the woman whose name I still didn't know.

"I did," I said.

"Good." She nodded. "And good luck with your band."

She started back into the kitchen.

"Wait," I said, standing up. "I still have questions."

She smiled at me over her shoulder. "I'm sure you do."

Fitz got on the phone after breakfast and found an acceptable replacement clutch at a junkyard for a reasonable price. Even got the guy to drop it by the service station.

We were up and running that afternoon, and even had time before the gig to check into a motel and grab some dinner.

The tour was a complete success. Not only did we actually make money on the door – which we never counted on in those days – but we even sold out of tee shirts, CDs, and download coupons.

That was the tour that launched us. Primed us, for the success that followed. Success built on the foundation of two albums worth of material. Mostly the songs I'd written that night in the Little Night's Sleep bed and breakfast.

I made sure to thank Puffer in the liner notes.

NIGHT OF THE HOGTIED ALIEN

Among the many strange and silly things that cats do, one of the strangest is surely their habit of tearing around a house or apartment, ardently in pursuit of nothing at all.

Well, nothing that we humans can perceive, anyway.

I'm not the first writer to write about this, nor will I be the last, I'm sure. But I was thinking about this little habit of theirs, and wondering what were some of the odder possibilities for why they did it.

In their little kitty minds, they're after something. Accomplishing something. And sure, on a purely mundane level, it may just be exercise, or hunting practice or something along such lines.

But where's the fun in that?

NIGHT OF THE HOGTIED ALIEN

My cat doesn't just judge me. I think he grades me.

I'll never see the report card, of course. Heck, I only recently found out the truth behind the way he'd watch me. Study me. The way he'd suddenly run off into another room, chasing something I couldn't see...

I adopted the little gray ball of puff from a rescue shelter about six months ago, when they set up shop for an afternoon in the back of a pet store. One of those big, chain stores, but not set up for pet adoptions full-time, so it smelled more like dry dog food than animal fur. And I had plenty of time to think about that smell because I had to walk past aisles and aisles full of the treats and toys I'd have to buy for my new dog.

And I *was* planning to get a dog. New best friend to keep my spirits up after a break-up. Beagle if they had one, Lab if they didn't. I could hear all kinds of excited barking in the back corner where the dogs were corralled, along with the occasional squeal of happy children picking out their new best friends.

But to get to the dogs, I had to pass through the feline gauntlet. Stacks and stacks of cages full of kittens. Kittens romping, kittens sleeping, kittens trying to mew loud enough to be heard above all the others. And running up and down the gauntlet, more children trying to see every one of those kittens.

I remember there was this one little girl with long natty hair, her brown eyes so wide they might have popped right out of her head. She kept darting back and forth between three cages, unable to make the biggest decision of her young life.

I was just past her when a gray paw reached through a cage door, trying to get to me. Me. Not any of the half dozen children scampering back and forth. Not the harried parents trying to keep those children under control.

Me.

At the other end of that paw was a gray cat – young, but too big to be a kitten – pushing to reach me and meowing like the world was coming to an end.

Like a fool, I stopped walking.

Suddenly the little brown-eyed girl was there, gasping. "He wants *you*. You're so *lucky*."

I thought about telling her that the cat was probably just reaching for the biggest sucker, but I took a good look at cat instead. Short, silky gray fur, but black specks across his nose and down his back. The tag on his cage said he was "almost" purebred Russian Blue. Poor thing probably ended up there over an almost, and with everyone around me wanting a kitten, the poor guy might go un-adopted.

That was the official story, at least. These days, well, I wonder.

Anyway, now that the cat had my attention, he went full bore. Both forepaws through the cage bars now, and both aimed squarely up at me. Not down at the little gasping girl, but up at the huge guy in denim and flannel, with the shaggy red hair.

I had to pick him up. And then I was sunk.

He snuggled right up under my chin and purred like an outboard motor. I never had a chance.

The little girl started giggling. Great big guy like me with a little gray cat tucked into my bushy red beard, kneading and burrowing for all he's worth. Soon I was surrounded by children, all laughing in what I'd like to think was delight.

An underpaid young woman in a nametag tried to tell me I wasn't supposed to bond with the cats until I filled out the paperwork and got approved for adoption. I told her to tell that to the cat.

Took him home that day. Named him Butterfield. Butter when he's sweet. Butt when he's not.

He fit right into my little apartment. I have a one-bedroom place, furnished piecemeal through thrift stores and Craigslist. Most of my furniture looks like it'll fall apart if a big enough semi rumbles past, but that hasn't happened yet. (fingers crossed) Pressboard dining room table, and pressboard bookshelves overstuffed with paperbacks. Mismatched plates and glasses and silverware, but most of the time I eat my frozen dinners off of paper plates.

I do have a king-size mattress, with matching redwood nightstands, while most of my friends are still sleeping on futons. So there's that.

My ex-girlfriend, Richelle, used to claim that most of the place smells like "dude," so while we were together I kept a "summer breeze" air freshener in my nightstand, ready to plug in on the nights she slept over. Least I can do.

Butterfield took to the place immediately. I set the cardboard carrier he came with down on the thin, puke brown carpet inside my front door and opened it up. I'm not quite sure what I expected. Maybe something skittish. But Butterfield leaped right out and began sniffing everything, bedroom to bathroom to kitchen.

I didn't notice any odd behavior that first day. But I hadn't been paying strict attention either. Everything he did was cute, from chin-marking the off-white walls to pulling at the carpet to stretch his claws.

Looking back now, I think I remember him checking out my bookshelves. At the time, it just seemed he was looking for places to climb. And Butterfield does love high vantage points. But these days, I wonder. Was he looking for specific titles? General themes? Did I get points for having Octavia Butler books? Lose points for not having any Frank Herbert?

I don't really know. And Butterfield was my first cat, so all I really knew about feline behavior was what I could read on the internet when I could get past the pages and pages of memes. He seemed to be settling in just fine, and I thought that was a good thing.

And he was so attentive. Every time I did anything at all, Butterfield was right there, watching. Browsing the internet? There's Butterfield, parked beside the monitor. Frying up a burger? There's Butterfield, watching me season. Waking up in the middle of the night? There was Butterfield, curled up beside me, bright blue eyes open and focused on me.

Even when I was sitting on the toilet, there was Butterfield. Watching. At first, I thought it was weird, but after a while, I got used to it. I figured he just liked being near me. After all, I was the one who fed him, cleaned his litterbox, played with him, and held and petted him several times a day.

Not to mention I was the apartment's only other occupant, as far as I knew. If Butterfield wanted attention, I was pretty much his only option.

But then I found out the truth, last Saturday.

⁂

IT WAS PRETTY LATE, SOMEWHERE PAST TWO. I KNOW THAT MUCH FOR sure, because the bars were closed, and my friends had all gone home with their girlfriends. A few of those girlfriends had brought friends along to meet me and see if any sparks flew, but they might as well have been trying to start a fire in the rain.

Nothing wrong with me – far as I know, anyway, though you might do better to ask Butterfield – and nothing wrong with any of those girls. There just wasn't enough connection to go beyond a dance or two and a little current affairs talk. Nice, but not *nice*, you know? And I don't go in much for one-night stands.

So, yeah, I had a few still in my system when the cab dropped me off by my little apartment complex, but I could walk a straight line. And I didn't have any trouble picking out my building on only the second try.

How long it took me to get the right key and open the door doesn't ... look, I'm not denying I was intoxicated, all right? I admit, I could still smell the Johnnie Walker on my own breath. That doesn't make what happened next any less true.

"Butterfield," I called as I flipped on the lights and closed the front door behind me, "I'm home."

Butterfield was right there, as always, sniffing all around me the moment I came in the door and shoving his sides and shoulders against me for petting. Made me chuckle as I wedged off my tied sneakers. The way he sniffed, like he could tell everywhere I'd been and everything I'd done just by the way my scent had changed since I went out.

I scooped him up, letting him burrow under my chin and knead my beard while I told him about the club.

Yeah, I talk to my cat. That breakup was six months ago, remember. A guy gets lonely.

Anyway, I'd just finished lamenting the state of my dating prospects when Butterfield's head came up like he'd heard something I didn't. He started kicking for down. Kicking hard, like I'd been holding him too long or something. Barely let me lower him toward the carpet when he wriggled free of my arms and went scampering.

The booze and the lamentations had made me a bit maudlin, and here even my cat was rejecting me just so he could go tearing around my apartment like he'd lost what few marbles would fit inside that little head.

Well, not this time. I watched him run down the hall, claws clinging to the carpet to let him corner through the dining room and living room before jetting back down the hall and past me into the bedroom.

I had to know what he was looking for. I followed. And I saw movement in the shadows, in the corner of my bedroom. My bed was against the near wall, my closet on the left wall, and the right wall was a display of my framed, autographed *Lord of the Rings* movie posters.

On the opposite wall was the big picture window and the two

sliding windows on either side. I'd left the curtains open, so plenty of light came in from the parking lot sodiums.

Enough let to let me pick out three shadows that didn't belong beside the curtains in the far right corner. Little guys, maybe five feet even.

And *my* cat, my own little gray puffball, sitting primly, facing those shadows.

I reacted before I even made sense of what I was seeing.

"What the hell?" I yelled, and I charged.

Four steps to cross the room. Time enough for two shadows to vanish, but the third was still there as I attempted an untrained flying tackle.

I have a hard head. If I had any doubts about that, they were assuaged when my skull punched a hole in the drywall. But the scotch was with me, and I missed the studs. I also didn't feel it. Not right away, at least.

And my arms, they were wrapped tight around some asshole who had to have broken in. Some asshole my cat hunted down for me. Like a good kitty. The asshole was slippery though, writhing like a snake and trying to get away.

So what my head could do to a wall, I tried to do to the asshole. I slammed my forehead into his.

Still not feeling it, so I did it again. And again.

The writhing stopped.

Satisfied, I dragged my home invader into the hallway light.

He wasn't human. If "he" was even the right designation. But I was drunk, and if this ... thing ... was a he, then I felt better about beating him unconscious. So I made a snap decision and decided my home invader was male.

He also had pale green skin, and stood about five feet even. Humanoid, but he couldn't have weighed half a potato chip. Skinny arms, skinny frame, not a lock of hair on his head or a stitch of clothing on his body (which had no, ah, visible equipment of any kind). His nose was lumpy, and my first thought was that it had been broken a couple of times.

Butterfield was there, pacing all around us and tail whipping back and forth as though this were the most distressing turn of events he could possibly imagine.

I probably should have called the cops. Or maybe the feds. But I wasn't thinking my most clearly. I just grabbed the terrycloth sash from my dark blue bathrobe and hog-tied the alien before carrying him to my saggy brown living room couch and depositing him there.

Butterfield followed and jumped onto my decrepit steamer trunk coffee table.

Little alien bastard came around right about the time that all these blows to my head started to ache. I came back in from the kitchen, swallowing a handful of ibuprofen and carrying a half-drunk glass of water when I saw that his eyes were open.

His eyes had whites, but they were green-tinted, and his irises were a mix of yellow and red. His pupils were vertical, and he had a second, black eyelid inside the outer, green one.

A wave of cold ran through me that sobered me up fast. Those were cat's eyes. And this alien was looking at Butterfield. Butterfield was staring right back into those eyes, eyebrows and ears twitching.

"How's your head?" I said.

The alien looked up at me. Eyes as mysterious as any cat. Couldn't tell if the alien understood. But I figured he could. If generations of sci-fi television shows had taught me anything about aliens, it's that they all speak English. If properly motivated.

"Gave you a couple of pretty good whacks there." I tapped my forehead, and didn't have to fake the wince that followed. "Got some ibuprofen or aspirin, if you want it. If it'll do you any good. Happy to give you either, or just a glass of something. But that'll only happen if you'll talk to me."

Nothing. Every bit as blank an expression as Butterfield could get. Butterfield, whose tail was still twitching so hard I expected him to achieve liftoff.

"If you can talk to me, I can give you something for your headache. But if you can't talk to me, I guess I'll just have to call the feds. Air Force, maybe."

"Water. Please." The alien's voice was soft, and high.

I nodded and fetched a glass. As I came back in, the alien had shifted to sit on his knees, even though his hands and feet were still bound behind his back.

"If you could untie me..."

I didn't say anything. I just brought the glass to the alien's lips and tilted so he could drink.

I set the glass down beside Butterfield, who started to drink from it. The alien wasn't the least bit disturbed.

I sat on the steamer trunk. Butterfield let me scratch him behind the ears, but he wasn't about to purr.

"He likes you," said the alien.

"I'd say he likes you too. Want to tell me what's going on?"

"Please, just let me go."

"You can tell me or you can tell the world. I might call the feds. Or the Air Force. Or maybe I'll just show up at a news station with you in tow. Make a great story."

Butterfield's head came up, and in the same moment, so did the alien's. Butterfield went tearing back down the hall.

I HAD A FEELING I WASN'T GOING TO LIKE WHAT WOULD HAPPEN NEXT.

I grabbed the bound alien and hefted him with both hands. I ran for my kitchen. My kitchen's not big, and it's not well stocked. Maybe three feet of white, speckled linoleum one direction and eight feet the other direction. Fridge, stove, microwave and cheap cabinets masquerading as white oak. White speckled Formica counters, all stained with old food, and some of those stains have been here longer than I have.

I could have grabbed my butcher knife. I could have grabbed my pizza cutter. Heck, I could have grabbed the cold pepperoni pizza from the fridge. But what *did* I grab?

A bottle of dish soap.

No, I don't know why I did it either. Maybe because it was green liquid and these were green aliens and... I don't know. I panicked. Okay?

Anyway, I'd just picked up the dish soap when two more aliens stepped to the edge of my kitchen. Butterfield darted between us, pacing and twitching his tail like he was sending an intense message in Morse code. The aliens had wicked looking pistols in their hands. Sleek, chrome jobs that looked like they shot lasers or something.

"Let him go," said one of the aliens.

Him. I knew it! I almost did an Icky Shuffle then, so maybe I wasn't quite as sobered up as I thought.

But they raised those pistols.

I held the bottle of dish soap to the bound alien's right nostril, hand poised to squeeze.

"I'll do it. I swear." I almost followed that with "I'll wash his mouth out with soap" but chewed the words down through a grin that I hoped looked menacing.

They took aim.

I started tilting the bottle.

Butterfield yowled.

All four of us – me and the three aliens – looked down at Butterfield. His face muscles were all moving, eyes and ears going like a series of tics.

"Is that true?" said the armed alien on the left, the one who'd spoken earlier.

"Is what true?" I said.

"As far as I can tell," said the bound alien, who did not look at all happy about the prospect of getting half a bottle of generic dish soap dumped up its nose. "What I've seen is consistent with the reports."

Reports?

"Fine," said the apparent leader alien. He lowered his pistol. A moment later, his armed companion did the same. "You can lower your chemical weapon. Let's just talk."

I did.

The little bastards zapped me.

Yellow radiation engulfed me. It felt like ten thousand tiny feathers tickling every inch of my body. Every. Inch. My immediate reaction covered my kitchen floor in dish soap, but then a fit of giggles hit me harder than drywall. I'm not normally all that ticklish, but I dropped the bottle and the alien and collapsed to the slick floor.

I don't quite know what happened next. I was rolling and shaking and pounding my fist on the floor and laughing and giggling. Laughing so hard my eyes closed. Laughing so hard I had trouble getting enough air.

I laughed myself right unconscious.

I WOKE UP SOMEWHERE CLOSE TO NOON THE NEXT DAY. LYING ON MY kitchen floor. Covered in dish soap. Must have been soaking in it all night. And no, my skin wasn't any softer. Butterfield was curled up in a soap-free spot on the linoleum, next to me. When his eyes opened, he gave me the most sleepy-eyed innocent look he could.

But that look was a lie. I knew the truth now. Not that I had any evidence to back it up.

The aliens were gone. The sash for my bathrobe was back looped through its loops as though it had never been yanked out and used to hogtie an alien. Only one glass of water in the living room, as though I'd never brought in a drink for a hogtied alien. So no alien DNA in a glass, say, for human scientists to study.

In fact, no proof of any kind that I hadn't imagined the whole thing in a drunken stupor. Except that I wasn't that drunk that night.

I thought long and hard about my situation as I took a shower and cleaned myself up. I liked the idea of telling somebody. The feds or the Air Force. Somebody like that. But what was the point, if I didn't have a shred of evidence to point to? And plenty of witnesses saw how drunk I was leaving the bar?

I still had the hole in the drywall where I'd tackled the alien. And the moment I saw it, my head started hurting and sent me back to the kitchen for ibuprofen. A hole was no evidence. I didn't have anything

I could bring to anybody else. All I really had was what I saw. I had no other witnesses...

I turned and looked at Butterfield. He sat in the bedroom doorway, staring at me with that thousand-mile stare cats have. He could have been wondering why I wasn't petting him ... or he could have been studying my reactions for his next report.

Report! The hog-tied alien said something about reports.

"That's you," I said as I approached. I knelt down and scratched Butterfield under the chin. "You're reporting on me to the aliens, aren't you? Giving them *all kinds* of information. Aren't you?"

Butterfield, of course, said nothing. But he did purr. He was getting his chin scratched, after all.

It's been almost a week now. The first few times I caught Butterfield darting out of the room I followed, but I have yet to see any more aliens. Not even any odd shapes in the shadows. Maybe they're being more careful. Maybe Butterfield is laying a false trail, to get me to stop following until it's back to business as usual.

I did consider trying to find Butterfield a new home, but I just can't. He may be a snitch, but he's my snitch, and I still love the little guy. But now when I talk to him, I don't just tell him about my day or reassure him that he's a good cat. I talk about politics and current affairs. I mean, if he's reporting it all to the aliens anyway, I might as well try to sound smart. Maybe it'll help when the invasion comes, or whatever.

I have to say, though. It's kind of weird petting him now. Now that I know the truth. Like I'm brown-nosing or something. But it would feel just as weird to stop. To start treating him like a roommate or something.

I do sometimes wonder if I'd be better off if I'd gotten a dog, but probably not. I mean, who knows who the dogs are reporting to?

THE HERALD'S TALE

I enjoy folklore almost as much as I do myths. I like to read them, and I like to write my own takes on them. This story is one of those.

There's a classic folk tale called "The King of Cats," about a man who witnesses a feline funeral, and what happens afterwards.

I won't spoil the folktale for you here, but I was never quite happy with the way it ended. And I knew that when I wrote my own version of it, I'd have to do something about that.

I'm afraid that's about all I can say without spoiling the story. If you're already familiar with the traditional tale, I hope you don't mind the liberties I've taken with the ending.

THE HERALD'S TALE

IT DIDN'T START WITH THE FUNERAL. WHEN I THINK BACK TO THAT DAY, most of the time I think of the funeral first, but that wasn't the way it started. Not for me. Not really.

My career was just taking off as a writer, in those days. In every respect. Magazine editors were finally buying my stories, instead of just sending me personal rejections. Readers were buying the first book in my trilogy, and clamoring for the next. And I'd found a rhythm at my writing desk. I could just sit down, and the words started flowing.

In fact, that was why I started taking walks twice a day. Sure, overall health was a consideration, but I needed to make myself take breaks from the typing or risk some kind of repetitive stress issue.

I was living in the hills of southwest Portland, then. Nice neighborhoods, but even better hiking trails. So numerous that most trails didn't have parking lots. Just little entrances, tucked away in the middle of blocks here and there like private gateways into Faerie.

I used to get my best ideas on those hikes. I'd just let my shoes handle the details of walking while my mind wandered far and wide. Everything I saw or heard might be the leaping off point into another story.

Ironic, in that it was on one of those walks that I ended up in a story myself.

Spring in the Oregon Willamette Valley could be a crapshoot. Sometimes winter seemed to linger, pelting us with hail or freezing rain. Other times we might get an unseasonable heatwave.

But that year, that year it was actually just pleasant. Not too cool or too hot. Just enough clouds overhead to keep direct sun from becoming a problem, and just enough breeze that even a moderate amount of physical effort didn't make me sweat.

'Course, that might've been my bias showing. I grew up in the Bay Area, so while I had a fine appreciation for rain, days like that one felt like home on a primal level.

Absolutely perfect day for a hike, as a way to lead into my lunch break.

I wandered down the hill from my house, weaving between trees and parked cars. Like most of the hills in southwest, the nearby side streets lacked sidewalks. Fortunately, they didn't have the kind of traffic volume to make that a problem.

It was maybe half a mile down to the foot of the hill. Just long enough to loosen up the old tightness in my lower back – remnant of an old basketball injury – and get my legs and feet feeling ready to do some real hiking.

I crossed the street, turned left past Sub Hunt, the little mom-and-pop sandwich shop where I intended to stop on the way back, and then took a right onto a dirt path tucked between Douglas firs, for my hike.

Technically I was now in a park. But if this park had a name, I never saw it listed anywhere. Even the various map apps only listed it as a swath of green to navigate around while driving. I think it only really existed for hiking. Never even saw any bikers here, which was weird for a bike-heavy town like Portland.

Anyway, one of the reasons I liked to hike through this particular stretch of outdoors was the variety. Douglas firs might've been the primary conifer in the Portland area, but this hiking trail had sections of pine and redwood, too.

Not next to each other, though. Oh, no. They were separated by packs of deciduous trees, like oaks and maples. I'm sure the actual reason had something to do with root systems, but being me I speculated wildly about the arboreal politics of this area. Complete with the role of the songbirds, flitting from tree to tree, lobbying hard to promote their own agendas.

I remember I was just cooking up a short story about it all that day, as I hiked along. The one that became "Needling the Root," about delegations of western conifers that met in the hills of southwest Portland.

In fact, I was just passing through a section of maples, where the leaves were just really coming in, and I was trying to decide what the role of the underbrush was – especially the ubiquitous ferns and Oregon grapes – when I spotted five cats huddled together at a bend in the trail.

I'd say I grew up with cats, but really I grew up with cat. One. Amphitrite, or Amphi for short. Sweet little girl cat with short gray fur and a love of mischief. She came to live with us when I was three, and finally passed on around the time I graduated from college.

She was the one who gave me my love for cats. Taught me that when cats feel safe and loved, they unleash their goofy side.

When we had guests over, she was mysterious and distant. A beauty they could admire, but not touch.

The moment guests were gone, she flopped on the floor in front of me, belly up, and would make this sweet, trilling meow until I rubbed her belly.

My parents didn't want another pet after Amphi died, but I couldn't resist. Soon as I'd gotten my own place, I'd gone straight to the shelter. And I'd shared my home with a cat ever since.

And among the things I'd learned about cats over the years was this – five cats huddled together was a strange sight.

It would have been one thing if they'd been litter mates, or something. But they didn't look related. One, the oldest, was a Siamese with chocolate points that I pegged to be over ten years old. Two were tabbies, one gray, one orange. They looked like adults, but I was pretty sure the orange tabby was younger by a year or two. One was a Russian blue, fit and strong and just out of kittenhood. The last was a Persian kitten, complete with that poor, smushed little face.

They weren't quite shoulder to shoulder, but they were gathered around something with their heads close together. None of them were making territorial sounds. None of them were posturing. There were none of the signs of the incipient catfight that I might expect.

In fact, if they were communicating at all, they were doing it in little movements of their eyes and ears and whiskers.

I never could sneak up on a cat. Though I'm not sure if that's my own failing, or just a statement about how perceptive the little buggers are.

Either way, I got about two quiet steps closer along the trail before the Siamese snapped to attention, eyes locked on me. She – I think it was a she – snorted, and the other four took off into the underbrush in different directions.

Well, they hadn't been huddled around a mouse or bird. I could tell that much immediately. No dead prey, or any object I could spot where I stood.

The Siamese glared at me for a moment longer, then turned and sashayed into the shelter of a fern. But as she left, her tail took a swipe at the ground that didn't look accidental, but didn't look like a statement about me, either.

No, a statement about me would've been more likely to come as a thump than a swipe. And maybe it was just because I was in story-telling mode, but I quickly convinced myself that the cat had been trying to erase something.

I hustled over. Sure enough, it looked as though something had been sketched in the dirt, then swiped at. It looked to have been a symbol composed of a handful – or rather a pawful – of quick claw slashes.

What else could it have been but a message?

I didn't write "Needling the Root" until a good two years after the day of that hike. Not because I didn't like the story idea, but because the events of that day shoved the whole concept of coniferous delegations straight out of my head.

As I wandered along the trail after sighting that first, five-cat gathering around what might have been a feline symbol of some sort, my focus was all about cats.

Every rustle I heard in the underbrush might've been another cat, delivering this strange message. Every small animal sighting out of the corner of my eye looked more like a cat than a squirrel or a raccoon. Every time the birds took off suddenly from their perch, I imagined they were responding to the movements of cats unseen to me.

The weirdest part about all of this? I was probably right.

Normally I'd've only gone maybe a mile and a half out along the trail. Enough to make the hike about three miles round trip, which I considered justification to have a couple of chocolate chip cookies with my lunch sandwich.

My second actual cat sighting killed that idea. This time it was only two cats, both tabbies, just off the trail maybe a dozen feet. They'd split before I reached them, but once more I saw evidence of some kind of feline symbol, sketched in the dirt.

Still partially wiped away. Still possibly my imagination, in terms of any connection to that first group of cats. But similar enough to merit more investigation.

I passed that kind of thing two more times over the next mile or two. And I know that, in my mind, I was still playing with those scratch marks in my head. Taking the little bits I could figure out about them with each sighting, and trying to jumble them together to make a coherent sigil.

But nothing was coming together. Whatever they were sketching, it wasn't a bird or a mouse, not a dog or a coyote or raccoon, not a can or bag or anything else I could think of that might be important to a local cat, either stray or domesticated.

I do know that after a certain point, I stopped seeing groves of deciduous trees. Around then, I found myself wondering when I'd last seen any tree that wasn't a Douglas fir. The underbrush had unified as well, now almost entirely either ferns or Oregon grapes.

I hadn't passed another hiker for quite some time. Not even the regulars, out walking their dogs at lunchtime.

That was enough to make me stop in the middle of the trail and wonder. I couldn't hear any cars. Not that this was a high-traffic area, but I5 wasn't all that far away. It was rare to be able to stand still and listen for more than maybe thirty seconds without hearing the distant roar of a truck's diesel engine, or the whine of a speeding motorcycle.

But I couldn't hear either. And I wasn't sure when last I did.

Weirder still, the birds weren't singing anymore. This time of year, the western meadowlarks should've been chattering up a storm. But where I was, the air had a hushed quality. No breeze. Very little sound.

I was struck by the oddest notion then. That this part of the woods – I had trouble still thinking of it as a trail, despite the presence of the dirt path I trod on – was a cathedral.

I found myself moving as quietly as I could, as much out of a sense of awe or respect as anything else.

I crept along. My focus split between those the possible meaning of those strange scratch marks, and trying to spot more cats, making them.

I came around a bend to my left, and ahead of me the path swelled wide into a clearing.

A clearing full of cats.

Dozens of cats. Every breed I could name, and several I couldn't. Cats of all ages and sizes. Obviously domesticated cats, well-groomed and wearing collars. Obviously feral cats, with their fur dirty or messy and a wary set to their posture.

All of these cats, gathered and looking up the trail ahead of me. Obviously waiting.

I stopped mid-step. Held my breath. Tried to still the sounds of my heart, which was pounding with amazement. My eyes rounded so wide that everything seemed to brighten a touch as my pupils expanded.

Still, one of the cats noticed me. The young Russian blue, from earlier. Or at least, it was a young Russian blue. I couldn't be sure it was the same one. He – or maybe she – made an inquisitive sound.

Now a dozen pairs of eyes fixed on me. Two of the feral cats, obvious fighters, started forward.

The Siamese from earlier – and something about her regard made me certain she was the same cat – gave a low growl, getting the attention of those strays, as well as the other cats near her. She thumped her tail once, and twitched her ears.

Apparently I was to be allowed to remain.

The strays resumed their places. Everyone turned back to watch the trail ahead of me. Of us, I suppose.

A somber looking tuxedo cat came down the trail, then took up a position in front of the assemblage.

I swear. For just a moment, I thought that cat was going to start speaking English.

She didn't, though. If anything, she seemed to be waiting, too.

Then I found out what they were waiting for.

Six young, strong black cats came down the trail. Carrying something.

A coffin. A cat-sized coffin.

That was too much for me. I turned and ran.

I COULDN'T RUN THE WHOLE WAY BACK. I JUST WASN'T IN THAT KIND OF shape. But in some ways, it didn't matter. Because although I had to have hiked a good three miles out, I swear my run/hike back covered less than two miles.

Either way, I didn't stop for lunch at the Sub Hunt. I pushed my complaining legs right back up the hill to my house, where I locked the door behind me.

Wasn't much of a house. Two bedrooms, a bath and a half, with a little, semi-furnished basement. But I trusted my walls to keep the outside out.

I sank down to the hardwood floor. Sweaty. Panting for breath. My heart acting as though I were still running instead of sitting against my front door.

By all rights, my stomach should've been clamoring for lunch. I was overdue to eat, and I'd certainly gotten plenty of exercise. All I can think, looking back, was that my stomach had been as weirded out as the rest of me.

I mean, yeah, keep Portland weird and all that. But this, this was weirdness beyond anything I was used to seeing outside of a story.

It was while I was still sitting there, gathering myself, that a cat came padding out of the kitchen to see me.

This cat, at least, I knew. Charlemagne. Char was my buddy. Found him at a cat rescue place when he was a kitten, almost six years ago at that point, and we'd been almost inseparable ever since. He didn't even mind being an indoor cat, which was a must for me. Too many raccoons and coyotes came through my neighborhood.

Char was that rarest of kitties, a male tortoise shell. His fur was almost entirely black, but with little spatterings of orange here and there, along with almost a halo of orange on the top of his head. Like a *pet here* circle.

When Char reached me, I scooped him up and held him close. Petting him and reassuring myself that I was all right and not insane or anything.

Char, for his part, just snuggled in and purred, loud and content.

Until I began telling him the story of my lunchtime hike.

As soon as I got to the part about the first gathering of five cats, and that one seemed to have scratched a symbol in the dirt, he stopped purring. He raised his head, and seemed to be listening intently while I continued.

When I got to the part about the coffin and what could only have been a funeral, he leaned his head back and yowled.

It was a sound of sorrow and loss, and it chilled my blood.

I didn't resist when Char jumped down to pace the floor in front of me.

"What's wrong, Char?" I asked finally. I don't think that, even then, I really expected him to answer me. It was just that I always spoke to Charlemagne as though he could understand me.

But this time, he stopped pacing and looked up at me.

"That funeral," he said, and now my skin joined my blood in feeling icy cold.

Char was speaking to me. In English. With a surprisingly deep voice.

I wondered if I was, in fact, having a psychotic break.

But Char kept talking.

"That funeral can only have been for my father." He sighed. "Which means I am now the king of cats, and I've got a lot of work to do."

He turned, buffed my knee, and ran out of the room.

I was on my feet in a flash, adrenaline forcing life into tired muscles.

I followed Char through the kitchen and into the family room, where he ran into the fireplace and vanished up the chimney.

And just like that, he was gone.

I stumbled to a vague sitting position, there on the stones of the hearth.

It was all real. The cats. The gathering. The funeral. I even understood what they'd sketched on the ground now. A crown.

It had all happened. It had all really happened.

But the only thing I could think about was that Charlemagne, my little Char cat, was gone.

THE NEXT WEEK WAS A ROUGH TIME FOR ME. I DIDN'T SLEEP. I BARELY ate. I couldn't even think about writing.

I started thinking that maybe I'd dreamed it all. That maybe Char had just gotten out because I'd left a door open or something. I mean, it wasn't the kind of thing I ever did, but certainly seemed more likely than that I'd witnessed the funeral of a feline monarch, and that my beloved cat had abandoned me to take the throne.

So I posted to the neighborhood app about a lost cat, and put up flyers all around the neighborhood. And for at least a dozen blocks outside my neighborhood, because cats can range pretty far. I also left my name and Char's picture with all the local vet hospitals and shelters.

Hell, I even made sure animal control knew that, if anyone found a male torty, he was most definitely missed and wanted.

I even heard from people a few times. And each time I dropped whatever I was doing and rushed out to check.

Of course, it was never Char.

Five days in, a friend of mine told me that I needed to face the facts. The cat was gone. The only thing I could do now was go to a shelter and get another cat.

There was logic to that. I knew it. But I wasn't ready to face it.

I didn't just want another cat. I wanted my Char.

It was the morning of the ninth day that I woke to a wonder.

Sleep, at that point, was nothing more than a fitful doze for maybe twenty minutes at a time before some tiny sound somewhere in the house yanked me awake.

And yet. And yet that eighth night, my body must've finally found some secret to shutting my brain down for a while. Because I didn't just startle awake. No. I rose slowly to a drowsy kind of consciousness. The sheets and pillows of my king-size bed rumpled and disorderly.

Sometime in my first dozen conscious breaths, it registered with me that there was a weight on my chest. A soft, purring weight.

My eyelids snapped open.

Clearly visible in the early morning sunlight, the sight of Charlemagne, my cat, curled up on my chest just the way he loved to.

By reflex I started petting him. Pleasure rippled down his fur, and he stretched his paws as he lay there.

I cleared my throat. His eyes stayed closed.

I scritched the area inside the halo – or maybe I should say the coronet – of orange fur on the top of his head. Char adjusted the angle to better suit him, and his purr got louder.

I cleared my throat again. He continued to try to pretend everything was normal.

I stopped petting him. He rolled slightly, exposing his belly.

"Oh, no," I said, "no belly rubs for you. Not until we talk about this."

His eyes opened the barest fraction, as though he were trying to gauge my sincerity.

I gave him a serious look.

He closed his eyes again.

"Did you at least miss me?" I asked.

That made him open his eyes. He rolled to his feet and purred loudly as he marked my chin over and over.

I chuckled against my will, then shook my head.

"Come on," I said. "You're not going to get away with pretending you don't speak English. Not anymore."

He sat back. Tilted his head as though confused.

"All right," I said. "Fine. You want me to believe I didn't witness a feline funeral. That I didn't come home and tell you about it. That you didn't then tell me you were the new king of cats, before vanishing for more than a week."

I gave a mock sigh and shook my head.

"And yet," I said, "I firmly believe all those things. That may mean I need to be institutionalized, which would mean I'd have to find you another home. I'd miss you, but—"

"Stop," Char said.

I, however, wasn't going to quit that easily. I was pretty pissed about his disappearing act.

"Heck, I'm still delusional. Maybe I should start posting about cat funerals online. Maybe others have—"

"All right, all right, you win," Char said, thumping his tail on my belly in annoyance.

"Good," I said. "Now tell me what the hell's going on."

Char sat primly on my chest, and bathed a paw while gathering his thoughts. Finally he spoke.

"It's pretty much like I told you the other day. I'm the new king of cats. I'm sorry I had to take off like that."

He stopped and buffed my chin a few times, and this time I let him, stroking his fur while renewed his marks.

"I hated doing it," he continued, sitting again, "and I missed you terribly. But I needed to go make appearances. Handle a few things about the transition."

He paused to reach down and wash his chest.

"In fact," he continued once more, "I'm going to have to do that periodically."

"No," I said.

"Charles," he said, "I don't have a choice in this. I don't like it either, but—"

"No," I said again.

"Sometimes I will have to deal with business myself," he said. "There are dignitaries to meet, disputes to settle. I have responsibilities."

"Then those responsibilities can come here," I said, tapping the bed with my finger, but hoping he understood I meant the house, not the bed. "We can set a schedule, and visiting cats can use the back door."

"You're not supposed to know about any of this," Char said, plaintively.

"Hey," I said. "I'm the one who saw the funeral, remember?"

"Technically you shouldn't have seen that either."

"Which I'm sure is what most of them thought," I said, "but that Siamese made them let me stay."

"Wait," Char said, and thumped his tail for emphasis. "A Siamese? Describe."

"Female, I'm pretty sure," I said. "Maybe ten years old? Brown points? Blue eyes?"

Char made this broken purring sound that, looking back, I'm pretty sure was a laugh.

In the moment, it was just confusing.

"Dad's vizier," Char said, finally. "That beautiful lady. I'll send her a bouquet of robins for this."

"Meaning..." I prompted.

"Meaning she's already put out the word that you know. Which means that what you're proposing will work. On one condition."

"Name it," I said.

Which is how I became herald to the king of cats. Six days a week, he's just my little buddy, Char. Playful, mischievous and affectionate as ever.

But on Thursday nights, I give up my good leather recliner to serve as his throne, and he holds court. A pair of big, hulking Norwegian forest cats serve as guards, and a stream of cats come in to have my cat settle disputes and make rulings.

I announce each one of them. And every time I do, Char gives me a wink.

ASK THE CATS

Some story ideas evolve naturally in a writer's head. Others spring out of nowhere and grab the writer by the throat. Still others are flung in the writer's face.

This story is that last type.

I was up on Whidbey Island in Washington, for a nine-day residency during my Master of Fine Arts program. Classes were intense, so break times helped preserve our sanity. During one such break, a handful of us went wandering along a trail through the nearby woods.

We didn't talk at first. Just enjoyed the warm summer air. The gentle songs of the local birds. The beauty of sunshine, dappling through the madrone trees.

Suddenly one of the other students turned to me and said, "Your next story should be called 'Ask the Cats.'"

I shrugged and accepted the challenge. Wrote it that night, after I finished my homework.

Took me a while to find the right home for this story, but when I did it became my first professional fiction sale.

ASK THE CATS

"Did you finish off the graham crackers?"

Irritated at the interruption of my favorite cop show, I looked up to see Pete pointing the empty box at me like a bible in the hands of one of those street corner pundits down by campus. Pete's not a big guy, but with one foot forward and his shoulders and jaw set, he looked ready to fight over this.

"Not me," I said, my hands coming up between us to distract him the crumbs on my tee shirt. "It must have been Carla."

That diffused his wrath. Carla was a Theater major and far better looking than a guy like Pete could hope to hold onto. He had told me just the night before over beer that he knew she would get bored and move on, that he just wanted to enjoy the ride. I was not convinced, though. I thought he worried about it more than he wanted to admit.

He narrowed his eyes at me and I tried not to feel those crumbs burning like guilt on my chest. He shifted his attention to Feynman and Schrodinger, his twin gray cats, sprawled together in their wicker basket. I turned back to my show, wondering what clue I had missed that had all the lab technicians jumping around like a family of pale-ontologists discovering a t-rex bone in their backyard. Then I heard Pete say something strange.

"Guys, did Tim eat the last graham crackers?"

I started to say something, but Pete was watching Feynman and Schrodinger. I expected to find myself scrutinized by enigmatic feline stares, but they were staring at something only cats can see. As far as I could tell, they didn't notice the question. Or Pete. Unless an ear twitch counts, or maybe a slight movement of the whiskers. Pete nodded.

"Next time, Tim, just throw the box out and add it to the shopping list, okay?" He went back to studying in his room before I could retort.

I looked back at the cats, and one of them met my eyes, timeless, but I'm never sure which is Feynman and which is Schrodinger.

Pete gave his cats the Magic 8-Ball treatment more and more often over the next few weeks. Who finished off the roll of toilet paper without changing it? Who put the empty milk carton back in the fridge? Who left those dishes in the sink? Sometimes it was me, but not always. Sometimes the cats were right, but not always. Carla thought it was cute, and she asked their opinions on broader issues of politics, the campus social scene, and even class selection for next semester.

I tried to write it off as one of those quirks that couples develop. It seemed like a good sign, a shared joke, even if Pete took it more seriously than she did. Or at least, Pete actually blamed me whenever the cats judged me guilty.

Toward the end of the semester, I lay collapsed in my bed when a pounding fist on my bedroom door jolted me to something like consciousness. I ached from too much caffeine, still sleep bleary and surrounded by chemistry texts in the light of my nightstand lamp, trying to puzzle out why the sound of electrons changing valence shells made me think of thumping on wood when the fist started up again, this time accompanied by a voice.

"Open the damned door, Tim!"

I started toward the closet before waking up enough to direct my stumble to the right door, jerking it open. I didn't get a word out before Pete spoke again.

"Is it you?" He forced words through a voice harsh with tears and fury. His jaw trembled like his white-knuckled fists, which were barely restrained at his sides.

"What...."

"Are you fucking Carla?"

My stomach fell through the floor, taking with it the last vestiges of my sleep. Carla had been around more lately, showing up before Pete got home and watching television or studying. Sometimes she rehearsed in Pete's room, or sat in there making phone calls.

"Answer. The. Question."

"Pete, I swear I never touched her."

"She just dumped me," he said, and the tremor that started at his feet now reached his voice, "for someone else." He closed his eyes, then fixed his dilated pupils on mine. "Tim, if I find out it's you...."

"I swear to God, Pete. It's not me." He stood there, staring, and only moments from swinging those fists. "Ask the cats!"

"What?"

"Ask Feynman and Schrodinger! They've been here the whole time. They'll tell you I never even looked at your girl."

Curiosity cracked its way through the haze of fury. He tilted his head in a shrug and stalked off the find the cats. I didn't dare move. I had just started wondering when my heart rate would slow when Pete came back down the hall holding our jackets.

"Buy an idiot a beer?" he asked with a sad attempt at a smile.

I let out a breath and took my jacket with my own attempt at a reassuring smile. As we walked through the cool, midnight streets toward the pub around the corner, I said, "I'm glad you have honest cats."

Pete looked at me sideways. "Tim, they're just cats."

THE SECRET OF CATNIP

I think the hardest part about having a pet is knowing you'll outlive the little ball of love and joy. With a cat, you're lucky to get fifteen to twenty years with them. And it sounds like a lot, but it goes by in a flash.

It was a lesson I learned when I was maybe eighteen. I was at the vet when I was told that my cat shouldn't have survived the drive there, and definitely wouldn't survive the drive home.

I was all alone when I had to say goodbye to him. I had to send the vet techs away three times because I wasn't finished. Darn near didn't survive the drive home myself.

I've had to say goodbye to a few others over the years since, and I can't say it's ever gotten easier.

I wrote this story not long after the loss of Dervish, twenty pounds of adorable Maine Coon affection. Just about the sweetest cat anyone could ever want to meet.

This wasn't an easy story to write. In fact, I think I wrote it from the cat's viewpoint because writing from the person's viewpoint would've hurt too much.

Still. Writing this story helped with my grief. If you've lost a pet of your own, maybe reading it will help with yours.

THE SECRET OF CATNIP

The day Midnight died, he almost didn't notice.

The sunbeam had been *just that good*.

Sunbeams were the perfect way to end a catnip jaunt through the room with the big white high-backed beds, the ones the two-legs sat on when they stared at their big flat box of colors and noise.

Catnip was fun. Made him feel like a kitten again, instead of the fifteen-year-old behemoth he'd become, with his short black fur stretched across his gloriously massive belly. Right ear permanently shortened by that scrap with a raccoon ... oh, sometime back.

Midnight was never a cat to waste time on reminiscence. The present, that was what mattered. And if he was no longer so swift and bouncy as the kitten he'd been, well, catnip helped bring back some of his lost youth.

The catnip had buzzed through him. Made him bounce and roll and pounce pounce pounce on the dangly thing at the end of Little Warmth's stick. Of the three two-legs Midnight lived with, Little Warmth was his favorite. She still giggled when they played, as she had when she was small and Midnight was a kitten. She had big blue eyes full of love, and long yellow hair Midnight got to bat at sometimes. And she still held him and sang to him and scritched all his favorite spots, just as she always had.

And after Midnight got to play catnip games with his favorite two-legs, that sunbeam under the giant rectangle window had been just perfect. The kind that made his fur ripple with pleasure as he settled down. Heat easing relaxation into his old bones as he rode out the tail end of his catnip buzz, purring himself to sleep.

So when Midnight rose from his nap in the lazy pre-dinner sun, he contemplated a snack and stretched the way he always did – forepaws sliding forward across the rough blue carpet until his shoulders pressed down that way that felt delightful. Then further still until he pushed his chest down past his belly and arched his hips just as high as they could go. Sleek tail high and proud. Then he dug his claws into the carpet to knead and stretch every tendon just so.

That was when Midnight began to notice that something wasn't right.

First, something was wrong with the carpet. It wasn't pulling against his claws the way it was supposed to. Why, he wasn't getting any of that good tendon stretch at all.

Second, he felt lighter. Lighter than he'd felt in years, even though he still had the expansive belly he was so proud of. So light he couldn't even feel that ache in his hips and knees that had been growing steadily for ... oh, for some time now.

Third, he could still feel the catnip buzz. That was even odder than the lightness, because catnip was an established part of Midnight's routine, and Midnight knew his routines well.

Once every seven days, Little Warmth would scatter some catnip on the carpet in the room with the big box of colors and noise. Wherever Midnight was in the house, he would smell it. Spicy and enticing as a whiff of mouse, enthralling as a treat in the hands of a two-legs. So good to roll around in. Even better to taste, it danced on his tongue when he licked it. Like the taste of wild grass and power. Something primal, as though the catnip spoke to some ancient version of Midnight, awakening it in the modern cat.

Little Warmth would watch and giggle while Midnight rolled and bounced, then she would stroke his fur and speak in the sweet voice she used only for him. Finally, she would take out the stick with the dangly thing and they would play until Midnight could play no more.

Then he would sleep in a sunbeam, and awaken sober and hungry.

But Midnight wasn't sober. He could still feel the buzz of the catnip making him bouncy. And he wasn't particularly hungry either.

Midnight looked around. The big, high-backed white beds that the two-legs sat on had some kind of white haze around them. Not like morning mist Midnight remembered from the days that the two-legs still let him romp around outside. Back before the raccoon. No, this mist had a slight glow to it. And it covered the pale walls too, and even the carpet. Everything had that haze.

And something was wrong with Midnight's nose. He should have been able to smell Little Warmth, and his food bowl, and that fake flowery smell that filled the house, especially around his sandbox.

But those smells were barely there.

Midnight needed help to figure this one out. He needed Little Warmth. He should have been able to hear her moving about, maybe in the room she slept in. She stared at other boxes in there. But the sounds, they were odd too. They echoed in a way he didn't like. As though he were in the tiny rain room where the two-legs tried to scrub away their smells.

Midnight didn't like any of this.

Except maybe the little buzz of catnip. That gave him some comfort. But still, he cried out long and loud for Little Warmth.

She didn't answer his first call, but that was not so odd. The two-legs, their ears weren't very good. So he called again. And again.

Finally Little Warmth came strolling into the room, carrying a tall, skinny, glass water bowl. That haze surrounded her too, thicker even than around the high-backed beds, but it didn't obscure her. As she entered, she was singing some little song that wasn't his so it didn't matter.

But she didn't come pick up Midnight or comfort him.

In fact, she walked straight past him to the sunbeam.

That was when Midnight saw his body for the first time. When Little Warmth crouched and reached to rub his body's belly, saying little nonsense things as she rubbed.

She figured out the truth at almost the same moment Midnight did.

And they both began to cry.

———

MIDNIGHT RECOVERED HIMSELF QUICKLY. DEATH WAS DEATH, AND nothing to be feared. He had brought it to his share of birds and field mice and tasty voles, back when the two-legs let him roam and hunt.

He had lived a full life, and he had always known death would come for him one day.

Truth was, Midnight had not been crying for himself.

He had been crying to feel such deep waves of sadness coming from his beloved Little Warmth.

Tears flowed down her unfortunately furless cheeks. Her nose sniffled and snuffled. Her voice broke as she held his body and tried to sing Midnight's songs.

Midnight went to her. Tried to put a paw on her leg to get her attention. That was his pick-me-up signal, but in the moment it only needed to say "Here I am. My body is not me. Here is your little Midnight."

But his paw passed through her leg with barely a pause. And Little Warmth didn't feel him. She didn't look up from the body of Midnight Past to the ... whatever Midnight Present was.

He needed to try harder. He lifted both forepaws to her leg and bellowed his where-are-you meow.

Nothing.

And Little Warmth was crying even louder, uttering small broken words, her sweet face turning red.

She plopped down on her butt on the blue carpet and fell backward, weeping as she cradled Midnight's body against her bosom as she had so many times. So much sadness flowed from her now that it almost overwhelmed Midnight. He wanted to cry for her too. To cry for the sadness he could not abate.

But the first moment of shock had passed, and now the catnip would not let him weep. It buzzed through him. Forming a layer of bounciness between Midnight and the sadness. But it gave no comfort now. The buzz was wrong. Vile. Catnip was a thing of joy, a little gift from Bast to the cats of the world, to remind them that deep down every cat is wild. That, unlike dogs, cats had never been tamed into obedience. That cats lived with the two-legs because they chose to.

Catnip was bliss. And this was a time of sadness.

So Midnight tried to shake off the buzz as Little Warmth lay there, crying over his body.

He jumped over and over his favorite two-legs, trying to work off the buzz as she wept. But he was so light now that the leaping took no more effort than the landing, and that scarcely required him to bend his now-pain-free joints.

He ran around her, and leaped, and pounced, and called out, but nothing seemed to break through those waves of sadness.

Finally, Little Warmth sat up, still holding Midnight's body as though he were still in it. She drew a few deep, shuddering breaths. Said a few things that sounded sweet but made her sob and squeeze her eyes tight.

That was too much.

Buzz or no buzz, Midnight put everything he had into one more meow. He reached deep within himself and let out a cry louder than the one that had chased off the Interloping Tabby some years back.

And for a moment – just a moment – Little Warmth stopped crying.

Her head came up, and she looked around the way the two-legs do when their weak ears can't tell where a sound came from. And then she said the one word he recognized.

"Midnight?"

But then she looked down at his body in her arms and shook her head, tears flowing down her face anew. She closed her eyes and shook her head harder. She said something else. Something dismissive sounding.

Little Warmth got awkwardly to her feet, and carried Midnight's body out of the room. He trotted along after her into the kitchen, where he could hardly hear her bare feet pad on the smooth floor that tasted fake and slick and lemon-but-not-lemon from the residue of the smell-ridder than the two-legs wiped across it.

Little Warmth picked up her tiny box from the cool stone counter, the one Midnight wasn't supposed to walk on, but did all the time anyway.

Midnight recognized the small, thin box she picked up. It was the one she played with and stared at more than any other box.

She held it to her ear and started speaking. But that was a two-legs thing. Whatever she was saying, it didn't matter. Not really.

Because Midnight realized three things.

First, Little Warmth had heard him call out, no matter how she now pretended she didn't.

Second, Midnight could no longer feel the catnip.

Those two facts had to be related. Running and jumping and pouncing had done nothing to work the catnip through Midnight, but that one call had used it up.

Midnight said a little word of thanks to Bast for giving cats catnip. And for the little bonus it seemed that herb brought over and above its bliss.

Catnip gave Midnight a way to reach across death to Little Warmth. And that was good, because of the third thing he realized.

Without the buzz of the catnip flowing through his system, Midnight could feel a tug inside his glorious belly. A tug that made him want to find a tree and climb, climb, climb. Instinct told him he felt the pull of the next world. That his time in this place was limited now.

Soon Midnight would have to pass beyond this world to the next, where he would wait for Little Warmth and guide her to what would follow.

But if catnip could keep that feeling at bay, then maybe it could help keep him here with Little Warmth...

But then Midnight remembered the way his paws passed through her leg, even with the catnip buzzing through him. He could not nuzzle her, or bathe her arms and chin properly. She could not stroke his fur, or scritch the places he liked, or cuddle him close.

He would be nothing more than ... whatever he was. Between. And that would be wrong. The time had come for him to move on, and that tug was his reminder that what came next was waiting.

But Midnight had to say goodbye first. He could not leave his beloved Little Warmth so full of sadness. Had to see one more smile on her face before the pull of the next world grew too strong to resist.

He needed more catnip.

THE PROBLEM WAS THAT MIDNIGHT DIDN'T KNOW WHERE LITTLE Warmth *kept* his supply of catnip. Yes, there were little bits in some of his toy mice, but that catnip was all old and used up. He needed the *fresh* catnip. He needed the catnip that Little Warmth would scatter for him every seven days, before they played their favorite game.

But Little Warmth hid that supply.

That was Midnight's own fault, and he knew it. He had seen only a few years of this world when he found his first supply. A little crinkly transparent thing full of catnip. He had smelled it on the cool stone counter not more than a few steps from where Little Warmth now held his body.

Young Midnight had smelled the catnip through the crinkly barrier. That was the first time he leapt onto the cool stone counter in the kitchen. He'd needed only moments to chew through the crinkles to the catnip inside.

He'd found that supply in the morning, and still been bouncy when Little Warmth came home hours later. Big Warmth and Deep Voice were with her, and they were angry at the artistic way Midnight had scattered the catnip across the counter as he rolled in it.

But then, the two-legs had no appreciation for art.

Ever since, Little Warmth had hidden away the catnip, and stored it in something stronger than the crinkly clear stuff. Midnight had tried a few times to smell it, but his nose could not pick it up, even when he was alive and all the scents were right.

They were all wrong now. He could barely tell the signature musk of Little Warmth from the lemon-not-lemon of the kitchen floor or the fake flower smell of the air.

But the tug in his belly was growing stronger, and he needed to act fast.

Midnight ran back into the room with the big flat box of noise and colors. Today's catnip was still there. Good. He was afraid he'd slept – or died – through the screaming sucker, the one Little Warmth used to catch up all the catnip after their games.

Midnight sprawled his massive body across the floor and started rolling.

Nothing happened.

The catnip wasn't sticking to his fur. He wasn't getting the smell the way he should have. A ripple of irritation flattened his ears and worked its way down until his tail twitched back and forth harshly.

He tried licking the catnip.

Something.

It wasn't quite the same, and it wasn't as strong as he would have liked. He couldn't quite taste it. But when his tongue passed through the catnip – and it did, just the way his paws had passed through Little Warmth's leg – he felt an echo of the proper buzz and a diminishment of the tug in his belly.

Midnight licked it all up. Every bit of catnip he could find. The buzz wasn't all it should have been, but it was something.

But what could he do with it?

And then he had an idea. Just a little puff of an idea. Hardly a dust mote worth chasing, but he had to try something.

Midnight sat in the middle of the scattered catnip and reach deep down into himself. He thought of his love for Little Warmth. He thought of his love of catnip. He thought of everything that was good in this world and he put every bit of it into the loudest, longest meow he'd ever given voice to.

He held that sound just as long as he could, and as he did he felt the buzz of the catnip leaking away and the tug in his belly starting again.

And it was stronger now. Urging him to run, to jump, to climb to what came next.

Little Warmth came running into the room, astonishment in her sweet blue eyes. Her face still red and puffy from all her crying.

Midnight's heart went out to her. He hated seeing the glimmer of hope underneath her confusion. Hated the wave of sadness that he knew would follow. Hated most of all that growing tug in his belly.

"Midnight?" she said again. And she looked around for him, saying little words he didn't understand, though he felt their hope. Perhaps she felt his presence. Knew that some part of him sat nearby, had called out to her.

Midnight's claws were working now, even though he could no longer knead the carpet. He needed to grip this world. To hold onto it just a little longer. To fight that need to move on.

Her shoulders slumped when she could not find him. Nor feel him. And she retrieved the screaming sucker and caught up all the catnip. Midnight followed her, fighting for every step as she put the screaming sucker away, and his hopes rose as she stopped and blinked for a moment.

Then she started up the stairs with a purpose. Midnight followed hot on her heels, prancing and high-stepping the way he had so very many times before. The tug seemed pleased that he was climbing something, but still it pulled him to move on.

When she got to the room she slept in, she went to the tall chest where she stored her fur substitutes. She pulled open the top drawer. Midnight knew that drawer. He'd gotten in there once when she'd left it open ... oh, some years past. He knew it held soft things that carried more of her smell than any of the other fur substitutes she used to cover her unfortunately furless body.

She pulled out a small glass jar, and inside it Midnight could see the answer to all his hopes.

His stash of catnip! More than he'd ever seen before. Nearly enough to halfway fill one of his cans of food.

Little Warmth turned, but before she could take a step Midnight pounced. He pounced like the catnip was a bird and this was his last chance to catch one before being confined for life to the indoor world.

He passed straight through the catnip, mouth open wide. Trying to consume it all at once.

And in this between state he could do just that.

Midnight was vibrating now. The catnip jolted through his system like the joy of a hunt and the pleasure of a scritch and the warmth of a sunbeam and a full belly all at once, and then some.

The tug went away. As though it were gone completely, but Midnight knew better.

Midnight ran in front of Little Warmth, who was now walking back toward the stairs.

He reached down into his depths as he had before, and poured all of his love for Little Warmth into two things: one last purring meow (and the purr came easily through all that catnip), and one last attempt to leap into her arms.

"Midnight?" said Little Warmth, dropping the jar of catnip...

...and trying to catch him.

And for that one moment. She could.

For that one moment, that one final moment, Midnight was once more purring in the arms of his beloved Little Warmth. She was laughing and crying all at once and trying to say his name.

But before she could finish his name, the moment was past and her arms moved through him.

The tug came back with a vengeance. Too strong for Midnight to resist now. He had no choice but to follow it through the wall to a great oak tree that had never been in his backyard territory during life. The Tree Between Worlds.

And with one last laughing crying smile from Little Warmth to bolster him, Midnight began to climb.

SIGN UP FOR STEFON'S NEWSLETTER

Stefon loves to keep in touch with his readers, and loves to keep you reading. The best way for him to do both is for you to sign up for his newsletter.

Sign up at http://www.stefonmears.com/join

If you sign up for Stefon's newsletter, you get...

- Monthly updates about his publishing and travel schedules
- His latest news, in brief, and answers to reader questions
- A free short story for signing up
- List-only offers and occasional specials
- Plus a free short story every month!

ABOUT THE AUTHOR

Stefon Mears has been accused of being a cat himself. Stefon has more than thirty books to his credit, and he never stops writing. He earned his M.F.A. in Creative Writing from N.I.L.A., and his B.A. in Religious Studies (double emphasis in Ritual and Mythology) from U.C. Berkeley. He's a lifelong gamer and fantasy fan. Stefon lives in Portland, Oregon, with his wife and three cats.

Look for Stefon online:
www.stefonmears.com
himself@stefonmears.com

ALSO BY STEFON MEARS

Cavan Oltblood Series

Half a Wizard

The Ice Dagger

The Spell in the Blade

Spells for Hire

Devil's Shoestring

Zombie Powder

Spirit Trap

Dragon's Blood

The Rise of Magic

Magician's Choice

Sleight of Mind

Lunar Alchemy

Three Fae Monte

The Sphinx Principle

The Telepath Trilogy

Surviving Telepathy

Immoral Telepathy

Targeting Telepathy

Edge of Humanity

Caught Between Monsters

Hunting Monsters

Power City Tales

Not Quite Bulletproof

No Money in Heroism

Devil's Night

Portal-Land, Oregon

With a Broken Sword

Twice Against the Dragon

The House on Cedar Street

Stealing from Pirates

Fade to Gold

Sudden Death

On the Edge of Faerie

Confronting Legends (Spells & Swords Vol. 1)

Uncle Stone Teeth and Other Macabre Poems

The Patreon Collection Vols. 1-4 (Vol. 5 coming soon)